Father's Secret

By

Anna Wheelock-Niemela

STONEWALL PRESS

PAVING YOUR WAY TO SUCCESS

Printed in the United States of America

ISBN: Paperback: 978-1-948172-32-5
           eBook: 978-1-948172-31-8

Library of Congress Control Number: 2018937470

Stonewall Press
363 Paladium Court
Owings Mills, MD 21117
www.stonewallpress.com
1-888-334-0980

Contents

Introduction

Jonathan, son of Mary Simon, took a step back and silently surveyed his new sign: "Nathan Van Veer, Attorney at Law." The sign signaled his success in obtaining a law degree from the University of Michigan and success at an apprenticeship under the well-known lawyers Van De and Van Dann. The sign also showed his rebellious growing-up years against the man who had begotten him, Martin Van Vedder.

Jonathan chose his business name carefully. He chose to be called Nathan, Patty's nickname for him. And, he dropped his mother's family name of Simon and deliberately desecrated his father's surname of Van Vedder by dropping the d's. Thus, his new business name became Nathan Van Veer. The law firm he just left was known as "Van De- Van Dann" and Nathan had become the Van V. Nathan was also defiantly rebelling against God. He respected his grandparent's strong faith, but he could no longer embrace it as he had as an innocent child before he heard his schoolmates call him a bastard child.

By hanging his sign in a changing neighborhood in a changing all-American city Nathan hoped to elicit a significant change in his own life. The whole world was engaged in change, whether by an increase of knowledge or its discontent with sameness. Through television man received news of distant regions. Freeways replaced highways as they reached out to connect large cities. New reforms in Social Security and in the Department of Health, Education and Welfare brought hope to many. School integration laws caused a move of blacks into formerly all-white neighborhoods. Fast growth of the nation and world affected individual neighborhoods. Families moved out of homes they had occupied for generations, rather than stay and watch their old neighborhood encroached upon by change. This city was no exception, shifting and stretching in all directions.

Chapter One

Grief dragged Martin Van Vedder to depths of despair he never knew existed. First, Martin's parents passed to their eternal reward. Hilda and Peter Van Vedder immigrated as newlyweds to America from the Netherlands and settled along the Thornapple River in Michigan.

Martin reminisced of happier youthful days. It was singing weather the day he and his parents moved from their small cottage into a proper house, as his mother called it. Water dripped from the edges of the roof and the spring sun shone on muddy rivulets between patches of snow.

Martin and his father had worked many long hours on their new home. Martin, carpenter-apprentice to his father, showed a natural talent in his detailed carving of the woodwork and mantel. To christen the new house, Martin's mother, Hilda, placed her cherished wooden box on the carved mantel. It was the only link with her home across the sea. Hilda received the box from her parents on her wedding day. The box cradled Hilda and Peter's wedding license and picture, photos of her parents and most recently, American citizenship papers. Martin's mother snapped a picture of a proud young Martin with his father in front of their new house the day they moved into it.

Martin grew to be a handsome young man of medium build and muscled shoulders, blond hair, blue eyes and a determined, dimpled chin. His only seeming mar was a dark birthmark on his right knee.

Martin and his lovely Suzanne formulated plan to spend the rest of their lives in the house that Martin and his father created together. Then, without warning, the Death Angel snatched Suzanne from Martin. She was struck down by a drunk driver on her way home from work, a week before they were to be wed.

With Suzanne gone, Martin's life turned sinister. He remained in shock for days. He drew small comfort from his pipe and survived on bread and coffee. He no longer lifted a finger to care for his beautiful house, which held no meaning without Suzanne. Even his friends Dr. Perkins and Suzanne's brother, Frank Reid, could not get through Martin's shield of suffering. For a time they visited him regularly. But, they finally left him alone, not wanting to intrude on his grief with solicitations. Martin also closed his heart to God, blaming God for his losses.

Gradually, the nightmares that saturated Martin's nights subsided. But, the agony never left him. Eventually, he made a feeble effort to resume the remnant of his life. He started by removing the dust from his mantel. The aroma of freshly polished wood soothed his senses. He washed an accumulation of dirty dishes and picked up carelessly tossed clothes.

Martin moved into the yard and mowed the grass. The exercise brought color to his sallow cheeks. His steps became surer as he paced back and forth across the lawn behind the mower. He stopped to mop perspiration from his face with a sleeve and determined next, to trim the hedge.

An apparition of Suzanne appeared before Martin as he trimmed the hedge. Suzanne stood there with sun gleaming on her golden hair as she hesitated at the gate.

"Oh, Suzanne, my lovely Suzanne," he whispered in her ear as he made love to her next to the hedge. Waves of emotion washed away a portion of his grief. Martin released her and gazed deep into her eyes for her responding look of love. Shocked, he saw only fright. "You are not my Suzanne." He pushed the trembling girl from him. She fled. Martin stumbled toward his house, shaken and confused.

Martin came to his sense as morning light streamed in his window. He must have fallen asleep in his chair. Perhaps, black coffee would clear his aching head. In the kitchen, he splashed cold water on his face and set the coffeepot on the stove. He barely noticed that the coffee scalded his mouth and throat. Bewildered, he scratched the birthmark on his knee, and picked up a carving block.

Chapter Two

John and Celia Simon, German immigrants, lived a few doors from the Van Vedder place. John ran a repair shop and could fix almost anything, except his wife's broken heart. The birth of their only child, Mary, had been a difficult one and left their child retarded. Mary developed physically and enjoyed helping her mother with small chores around the house. Mary liked to watch her father work in his shop. John built a swing for Mary in a big maple tree outside his shop. There, Mary swung and watched the neighborhood children play, but she was never invited to join. Sometimes, Mary wandered down the street to watch the children play in another yard. Celia did not worry, as Mary never crossed the street. The neighbors all knew the Simons through John's shop.

One afternoon, Mary returned home with skinned knees and grass-stained dress. Celia bandaged her knees. But, Mary would not be consoled and cried herself to sleep. Celia chided herself for not keeping a closing eye on Mary. That summer Mary spent more time indoors with her story books an dolls, complaining of the hot weather. Occasionally, she went to sit in her swing. Evenings, she was most happy playing checkers with her father while her mother mended.

One lazy morning, late in the summer, Celia sipped a second cup of coffee and watched Mary play with her dolls. A new truth dawned on her and her heart skipped a beat. Her head spun dizzily at a new realization. "Oh, no," she moaned. "Mary, do you remember the day when you fell down and skinned your knees?" Mary looked up, her face full of fear. Celia put her arms around her daughter as if to protect her from harm, but it was too late. Gradually, she pieced together her daughter's story about the man who pushed her down. Celia tucked Mary into bed and sat by her until her sobs subsided into the smooth breathing of sleep.

Celia faced another fear. "How will I ever tell John? He will rant and rave." But, what could they do? They were poor folks, unrecognized socially in their neighborhood. "Who would take the word of retarded girl against the word of a respected citizen?" After much contemplation, she decided, "I will call Dr. Perkins."

Dr. Perkins closed the door to Mary's room. "John, I need to talk to you. You are a good man and have had your share of hardships. But, some people are called upon to carry a heavier load than others. You are a sensible man. I want you to listen and pray to God before you act." Dr. Perkins paused, wiped his glasses and looked from John to Celia. "Mary is pregnant," he announced.

The word exploded on John's ears like bellows on a spark of flame. "What?" John shouted! "Who is the scoundrel that did such a shameful thing to an innocent child? I will kill him! Children are supposed to be safe in this town."

"Hold on, John." The doctor reached to restrain John. But, John wrenched away. "Mary needs you. You cannot help her if you are locked up in prison for murder." Finally, Dr. Perkins' gentle persuading words penetrated John's perturbed brain.

John clenched his fists, fighting for composure while considering his next step. With heavy heart, he lifted his eyes to his wife's haggard face. He had thought Mary's handicap was the worst of their pain. Now, another distress tormented them. Dr. Perkins thought of his own infant granddaughter. He was not so sure that he might react in the same way. "What are we going to do, Doctor?" pleaded John.

"Trust in God. Remember he never gives us more than we can bear. Mary is healthy girl and I will keep a close eye on her. You and Celia can help her raise the child, if you wish to keep it. Otherwise, I will help you arrange for an adoption."

"But, who is the man?" demanded John. He could not bring himself to say, "father of the child."

"I am not sure, but we cannot accuse Martin without proof". At the mention of Martin's name, John's head jerked up in surprise. The doctor continued. "Martin's grief of losing Suzanne may have confused his rational thinking. I will talk with him tonight. You stay away from Martin until I talk with him, do you hear?"

"Yes, mumbled John and retreated out the back door to his repair shop. Everyone knew Martin's tragedy and sympathized, but John hardly expected this of him. John remained in his workshop until after Celia retired to their bed. Too full of emotion to talk, Celia reached out to him and they fell asleep locked in each other's arms, their hearts full of anguish again for their only child.

Chapter Three

"Good evening, Martin," greeted Dr. Perkins.

"Hello." Martin raised an eyebrow in question. Dr. Perkins had not visited him since he was rebuffed after Suzanne's death.

"May I come in?" Martin moved aside and motioned toward a chair. Martin showed little emotion. However, the once neglected house appeared neat and comfortable again. Dr. Perkin's neck muscles bulged agitatedly. "Martin," he began, "we have been friends for a long time." Martin nodded, taking a puff from his pipe. "I will come straight to the point. I just came from the Simon place."

Martin held the doctor's gaze and blew a smoke ring. Dr. Perkins continued, "I checked on young Mary. She is pregnant and pointing a finger at you, a serious accusation. You have suffered enough grief without this. Of course, it is her word against yours. Her father's fury may cause him to act irrational, but, to accuse you, Martin. Say the word. Deny it," he begged. "I will believe you", Martin did not blink. He made no move to acknowledge or reject the accusation. Dr. Perkins waited for Martin to respond. "Your silence condemns you. I am sorry, friend." Dr. Perkins laid a hand on Martin's shoulder as he left. Martin had come to a crossroads and did not have the courage to do what is right. Now, he must abandon forever that which he held most dear, his home. He had already abandoned God.

Martin finished his pipe, hit it against the palms of his hand and stuffed it into his shirt pocket. Deliberately, he went to his bedroom, took down two new suitcases, saved for his honeymoon. "Well, I will begin a new life," he said bitterly to himself, "not as a married man, but as a fugitive." He emptied drawers into one suitcase, filled the other with clothes from his closet, surveyed the house and stopped by the mantel.

Tears trickled down Martin's cheeks as he picked up his mother's cherished box and wrapped it in a shirt, grateful his mother did not have to witness his wantonness. Martin shoved the suitcases into the car trunk, selected some tools from the workshop and said good-by to the rest. He extracted his driver's license from his wallet and watched it float away. In the car, he glanced in the mirror. He no longer recognized himself.

"Good-bye, Martin Van Vedder," he whispered hoarsely. He paused a moment to think then announced, "Hello, Mark Wagner."

Chapter Four

Loneliness had been a way of life for Nathan Simon since childhood. Rebuffed by other children, Nathan learned to keep himself aloof. He had survived the minor jolts of growing up. He would survive now. He was too busy to be very lonely.

Petite Patty Perkins, red-haired granddaughter of the local Dr. Perkins, was his sole playmate and devoted friend. She understood him more than any other person. Together, they climbed trees and exchanged dreams. From their vintage place high in the trees, they observed local residents coming and going from the post office, focal center of town. Within view, other children played on the school playground. "Someday, I am going to be postmistress and give people letters from friends far away," announced Patty.

"I want to be a lawyer," confided Nathan. "It will take me long time to earn enough money to go to college. I cannot expect Grandfather to send me. He deserves a rest."

"Nathan the brilliant lawyer," cheered Patty, his devoted friend. Patty could squelch any of his outbursts of anger with a stamp of her tiny foot and a scowl from flashing eyes. She looked so serious that Nathan invariably ended up laughing.

Together they laughed with the sheer joy of laughing. Then Patty would burst into song.

Occasionally, Nathan and Patty ventured down the street to the forbidden Van Vedder place the neighborhood children called the haunted house. The sudden and mysterious disappearance of Martin Van Vedder earned the property this unfavorable reputation. To be forbidden intensified the curiosity of the children.

Dr. Perkins, former friend of the Van Vedders, bought a couple goats to graze there. The goats kept the growth of grass down and protected the property. To imaginative children the bearded goats with horns appeared as ghostly demons. On one exploration of the grounds of the Van Vedder place, Nathan and Patty found a smoking pipe and hand-carved wooden toys. Later, Nathan realized the house belonged to his father and grandfather. When he knew of his origins, he lost interest in exploring the place.

Nathan never forgot the day Grandfather Simon brought him to Dr. Perkins' office and he learned about his father. The difficult explanation delivered by the kind doctor evaded the little boy's comprehension.

"Bastard," the hateful name he first heard from boys at school, burned in his mind. Rejection, repulsion and anger overwhelmed him. Nathan should not let hatred destroy his life. "Your father was my friend. I pray that someday common sense and love will draw him back. I know he would love you. I also am your friend, Nathan."

"How can you be my friend, if you were his?" Nathan had sobbed.

"I knew your father a long time ago. He suffered some tragedies that he could not cope with. Take this picture of your father. Keep it. Try to forgive him as your grandparents forgive you when you do something you should not," said the doctor.

For years, Nathan had lived in ignorant bliss without a father. Now, he knew a father existed; love and humiliation vied for his attention. "Why did he have to find out?" He tried to remember all that Dr. Perkins told him, but he could not forgive his father. Confusion reigned. Loneliness turned to bitterness.

Another fear gnawed at Nathan. Suppose some unknown evil inherited characteristic of his father surfaced in himself. Grandfather Simon counseled Nathan, "Concentrate on your own good qualities. You are a fine person, your mother's son and our grandson. And do not ever forget that you are God's son and he loves you. Do not get stuck in the past."

Chapter Five

Martin Van Vedder, alias Mark Wagner, ignored his surroundings as the miles sped by throughout the night. So much needed sorting in his mind. He arrived at a small town near the southern border of the state before his senses awakened. Checking the dials on the dash, he marveled that he had not run out of gas while his mind was in a state of stupor. He filled the gas tank and pulled over to a café, simply called The Coffee House.

Mark sipped a cup of coffee and observed his surroundings. He was a conspicuous stranger, void of family and friends for the first time in his life, and avowed it a most unpleasant experience. The smell of fresh-sawed lumber drifted in, reminding Mark of home and working with his father.

A group of jovial workmen entered for morning coffee. "Hi, Jenny," they called to the waitress.

"Hi fellows, I will be right with you." Jenny gathered up a tray of water glasses and waited to take their orders. Now that Mark knew the name of the waitress, he did not feel a total stranger. Stranger, he must find lodging and work. Mark could no longer allow himself to think of the house he and his father constructed together as home. He must stop at nothing to see that the past stay buried. Yesterday existed ages ago, and vague in his memory.

Mark paid for his coffee and a newspaper and left the café. Back in his car, Mark continued down the main street, turned and zigzagged his way along various streets. He noted the usual grocery, hardware, gas stations, fire department, school, churches, library and park. Mark parked his car and approached a park bench. He lit his pipe and allowed himself to relax a bit as he looked over the local Gazette checking ads for work and rooms for rent.

An elderly lady answered his knock and graciously showed him a small, but comfortable room. The room was furnished with a dresser, an easy chair and a small table holding a reading lamp. A large bed was covered with a homemade coverlet. "You are welcome to share meals with me", she suggested.

"Thanks," Mark replied. "I am not very hungry tonight. Perhaps, I could just have a sandwich in my room."

Mrs. Merrimills looked at him closely, and nodded. "That will be fine." Sometime later, Mrs. Merrimills gave a gentle knock and left a tray with a sandwich and tall glass of lemonade on the table. Mark chewed on the sandwich and drank the lemonade barely noticing the taste, but felt refreshed. Mark stretched out to pull his life together, he had knocked it down like a row of dominoes. He dozed fitfully, besieged with new nightmares.

It was the next afternoon before Mark aroused himself, showered and shaved. With pipe in hand, he went to sit on the front porch. Mrs. Merrimills appeared with a couple of tempting trays. She set one tray on the table next to Mark and took her own to her rocker. Mrs. Merrimills made an attempt at conversation. "I always enjoy eating out here in nice weather." Mark nodded acknowledgement. Mrs. Merrimills continued. "I know the feel of being a stranger. It takes time to become part of a new community. My husband and I came here several years ago and we enjoyed many good times. He died a year ago, but his memory is still fresh in my mind." She stopped and sighed.

Mark looked at her with compassion and said, "I am sorry. I also lost someone." Not only had he lost his parents and Suzanne, he had lost himself. Mark stood up, set his tray on the table and started down the walk. Martin was beginning to surface in his thoughts, and he needed to think as Mark.

Mark returned at dusk. Mrs. Merrimills read her Bible by the lone lamp in the living room, reminding him of his parents. A radio, her only human contact, played soft music. A worn carpet covered the floor and hand-crocheted doilies adorned each overstuffed chair back and arm. Mark hesitated to disturb the peaceful scene so tip-toed quietly to his room.

Mark picked up the newspaper and rechecked the work ads. An ad for help at the sawmill attracted his attention.

"Do you know about sawmill operations?" asked Sam.

"No, but I am willing to learn. And I am pretty good carpenter."

Chapter Six

Mark ventured out to acquaint himself with his new surroundings. He drove down one country road after another, past newly seeded farmlands and stands of fine timber. Cattle grazed on rolling hillsides. Shade trees and ample apple orchards surrounded comfortable dwellings.

Mark's old car coughed and wheezed as he rounded a curve. It coasted then rested at the crest of a knoll. Uneasiness engulfed Mark. He got out of his car, took a quick look over his shoulder and lifted the hood to inspect the damages. He knew this was bound to happen sooner or later. He just wished it had not happened so far from town.

Mark debated with himself what to do next. Perhaps, he should just abandon the car. Before he had time to make up his mind, he heard a vehicle approaching. A familiar knot tightened in the pit of his stomach. Oh well, if it was the police, he would just give himself up. He resigned himself to the fact that he would never be free from trouble. No sense praying now. He felt God had left him long ago.

Mark shuddered as a pickup truck passed and pulled over directly in front of him. Mark did not raise his head from under the hood until he heard a friendly voice, "Hi, neighbor, got a problem?" It was then that Mark noticed the truck was a wrecker.

"I guess this car is beyond fixing," Mark replied.

"I am Jim of Jim's Junk. Would you like me to tow you somewhere?"

"Well, I am not sure. I have a room in town at Mrs. Merrimills. Monday, I start work at the sawmill. Do you know where I can get a replacement for this piece of junk?" Mark thought that perhaps he would be harder to trace if his old car were junked and he drove another. He was hiding from himself more than deliberately hiding from the law.

"If you are willing," said Jim, "we can park this car in my junk yard. Then we can go over to Hank's used car lot. He won't dare give you a bad deal, seeing you are a friend of Mrs. Merrimills."

Mark walked around the car lot. Hank offered bits of information as he introduced various cars. Finally, Mark settled on one and they agreed on a price. Mark drove off satisfied with his new transportation and found Mrs. Merrimills sitting on the front porch. He honked and waved to her as she came down the steps. "Is that you, Mark?"

"Yes, my other car found its final rest at Jim's Junk. He helped me pick this one out at Hank's. Jim said that Hank would not dare give me anything but a good deal if he knew I was a friend of yours. You underestimate your popularity around here."

Mark held the door open. "Want to go for a ride?"

"I think I will. Let's get some ice cream for supper and celebrate." Now, that sounded like folk back home, thought Mark.

Monday morning, Mark arrived at the sawmill just as Sam, the foreman, climbed out of his pickup. He nodded at Mark. "Might as well meet the crew you will be working with," he said. "These two young fellows are Tom and Bart. Tom is Boss Bill's son. This tall drink of water is Joe, muscles here is Ed." On down the line he introduced Josh, Herm, Gill, Drew, Nate and Lew. Mark shook hands with each, noting their firm grip.

Sam handed Mark a hard hat. "Time to get to work." The noise and size of the saws surprised Mark as they reduced logs to boards in a matter of minutes. Sam assigned Mark to take scraps off the end of one conveyor belt. The next few weeks, he encountered a number of different operations and hazardous situations. Mark had always respected beautiful wood. Now, he held in high regard the men who turned trees into beautiful boards.

One dreary day, Mark's duties thrust him into one situation he would never forget. A bulging belt broke as it rotated. Mark ducked and dived for a far corner. The loose end of the belt whipped and slapped the wall with a fury. Mark cringed. Any moment life would be knocked from his defenseless body and he was not ready to meet his maker. Tension and hysteria built in him. The whine of the saws muffled his cries for help.

Sam, an alert foreman, noticed the malfunction immediately and ordered the operation shut down. However, the writhing belts whipped some determined last whacks at Mark. Mark remained motionless, cowering with arms raised over his head, his body drenched with perspiration. "It is okay to come out now," called Sam. Sam went to Mark and gently coaxed him. "The belt has stopped. Come, I will help you. Are you hurt?"

The slamming belt had brought all of Mark's problems crushing down on him at once, his parents' death, Suzanne's tragic death, his loneliness, the truth of Dr. Perkins' accusation and the loss of his personal identity. All this left him powerless.

Sam shook him gently. "Mark, are you hurt? Talk to me."

Sam's kindness seeped into Mark's consciousness and he allowed himself to be led to out into the fresh air. "Do you want me to take him to home, boss?" asked Sam.

"Yes, I don't think the belts hit him. You can explain to Mrs. Merrimills what happened. It will take us awhile to make repairs here."

"We are on it, boss," said Ed, grateful that Mark escaped the belts if not their fury.

Mark lay in bed with his eyes closed. He heard voices around him, but he could not respond to them. He heard the doctor say, "Let him rest. He has suffered an emotional, if not a physical trauma."

Finally, footsteps retreated and the door closed. He was aware of someone holding his hand. Then he heard Mrs. Merrimills' soft voice praying to God for his recovery. "Jesus, reach down and touch this wounded heart. Restore his faith in you. Help him to face his problems and make him ready to face the world. Help him to rejoice in your love."

Tears formed behind Mark's eyelids and flooded down his cheeks, washing away some of the pain. Mrs. Merrimills gave his hand a squeeze and said, "You will heal now, son." Quietly she left the room.

Under Mrs. Merrimills' kind attention, Mark regained his composure. And, the companionship and loyalties of the men at work became a stabilizing force in Mark's life.

Chapter Seven

Among friends, Mark Wagner began to forget Martin Van Vedder. He even dated Jenny the favorite waitress. Jenny dated several of the young men in the community. But Bart resented Mark's intrusion most. The previous summer, Bart escorted Jenny to the summer festival. He hoped to again this year. But, at Mrs. Merrimills' suggestion, Mark asked Jenny to accompany him. Jenny was delighted. Mark, a newcomer and rather mysterious about his past, excited her.

Summer and winter passed. Jenny and Mark continued their relationship and grew fonder of each other. Jenny and Mrs. Merrimills formed their own alliance. They had no family of their own. Jenny often confided in Mrs. Merrimills and accepted her motherly advice. When Jenny and Mark began making wedding plans, Mrs. Merrimills offered to share her home. So, Mark built a special apartment for Mrs. Merrimills in the back rooms of the house. Jenny and Mark occupied the front half. Together, they all formed a special family.

That June morning, Mark carried Jenny over the threshold and planted a kiss so firm and tender on her lips she thought her heart would burst with happiness. They honeymooned in a little cabin by Lake Michigan. In anticipation of their return,

Mrs. Merrimills placed fresh flowers from her garden on the dining-room table. She was more of a mother than landlord.

Mrs. Merrimills noticed Jenny's pregnancy symptoms before Jenny confirmed the news. Mark, proud of his son David, handed out cigars to his fellow workers and boasted he would one day leave the sawmill and set up a carpentry shop with his son. Mark remembered how he had helped his father, and other memories began to push into his consciousness that he could not control. So, Mark kept busy by carving his son's first cradle and toys.

The new parents swelled with pride as David cut his first tooth, said his first word and took his first steps. Jenny went back to work with Mrs. Merrimills as babysitter. Perhaps, the parents were too preoccupied with the child and forgot to tend to their own relationship. Accusing actions from both ended in arguments and sadness. Jenny could not pinpoint when the marriage began to deteriorate. But it must have been around their second anniversary and David's first birthday that Mark began drinking. He did not join the boisterous revelry of the boys at the bar, but brought his bottle home. He wanted to be alone. Somehow, he managed to keep sober enough to hold onto his job at the sawmill. This hazardous job left no room for mistakes.

Troubled thoughts from the past plagued Mark. He did not mean to shut Jenny out of his life, but how could he explain without hurting her? He dearly loved their son David, but somewhere another child, his child, was denied his love. That child was born of the agony of his first love, Suzanne. Would he ever know his child?

David started school and tensions mounted in the Wagner household. Young David listened terrified behind his bedroom door. He loved his parents and could not understand their arguments. Mark wondered how Jenny managed to put up with him as long as she did, even after the death of her dear friend and confidant, Mrs. Merrimills, or Grandma as David called her.

As a young child, David was well behaved and a good student. This was due largely to Mrs. Merrimills' influence. But as he grew older David skipped school and often got in fights. Mark and Jenny were called to school on several occasions. Mark knew that David and his friend Hal often tested their strength by wrestling, but always on friendly terms. Mark was proud of his son's endurance. But fights at school disturbed him. David had chosen new friends and began assuming their character. He became discourteous to his parents and broke curfew. Mark wondered if he was the cause of his son's unhappiness.

"Why, oh why, do I keep hurting the ones I love?" Mark moaned. He sat at the kitchen table with head bowed on his arms. In the other room, Jenny packed her bags to leave him. How could he have driven her from him? How could he bear to let Jenny go? Jenny had been his lifesaver in his new identity. His tortured mind could find no relief. He had no choice in losing Suzanne. But he had driven Jenny away.

Jenny sat on the edge of her bed; packed suitcases stood by the door. She found it difficult to believe her marriage to Mark, which had started with such promise, was now over. She had said good-bye to David before he left for school. She would miss him, but found herself unable to stay here any longer.

A knock at the door roused Mark. "That must be Fred, Jenny's new friend." Mark had driven her away into the arms of another that gave her comfort and treated her as a lady. Mark must bear the consequences again of his confused behavior. He could not bear the shame in front of his friends. He would take David away and begin again. This time there was no reason to change their identity.

Chapter Eight

To make life bearable, young Nathan decided to become a lawyer. He would find the man who had fathered him and bring him to justice.

Dr. Perkins considered how he might help Nathan to become a lawyer. However, he did not know the basis of Nathan's decision. The doctor's practice provided a steady income, but no great wealth. Perhaps, the offer of a loan to be paid back when Nathan set up his own law practice or an available scholarship might not offend him or his grandparents. This was the least he could do for an old friend. The doctor admired Nathan, a gritty fellow and a match to his own hot-tempered granddaughter, Patty. Nathan, a credit to his family, partially compensated for the suffering caused by his father.

In college, Nathan served on debate teams with girls, but discouraged personal involvement. Later, he escorted Cynthia, beautiful, petulant daughter of his former associate Mr. Van De, to social functions. Unbeknown to Nathan, Mr. Van De considered Cynthia a part of the contract when he joined the firm.

Cynthia, attractive in her own way, provided pleasant company. But Nathan still remembered the uncomfortable situation when he announced to Mr. Van De, "I am leaving the firm. Thank you for your support and mentoring." It was also a statement that he no longer held obligations to Cynthia. Mr. Van De's face registered surprise at Nathan's candor. Yet, he prided Nathan's fortitude in prevailing against him.

As junior partner of Van De and Van Dann, Nathan gained a certain amount of recognition. He matured into a favorable lawyer in his own right. Meticulous research and a force of persuasion springing from an inner energy won for Nathan the respect of his clients. Any tendency of temperamental behavior was directed toward his opponents in the courtroom.

Nathan Van Veer, formerly Jonathan Simon, found an upstairs apartment. Jake and Louise Dyke lived at the edge of one changing neighborhood. Affordable rent in this changing part of the city plus more clients, brought about by frustrations of change, prompted Nathan to settle here.

"We are happy to have another young person in the house after our daughter, Ellen, left us. She is a teacher now." Mrs. Dyke caught her breath then offered, "May I help you with your laundry? Just go through the attic room and down the back stairs. Bring your laundry on Fridays. I will have it ready for you on Monday."

"Thank you," said Nathan. He would miss his grandmother's help. "But in return," he said, "I will help you with small household repairs. I can tighten the screen door hinge and fix the loose porch railing if you are willing. My grandfather owns a repair shop, and he made certain I absorbed some practical learning before leaving home." Nathan checked himself. He did not want to give out more information about himself. This friendly woman caught him off guard.

"You are very observant. You will succeed as a lawyer," commented Mrs. Dyke.

A young black man pushing a lawn mower appeared around the corner of the house. "All finished, ma'am."

"Thank you, Arthur. Come, meet our new upstairs neighbor."

"Nathan Van Veer, meet Arthur Washington, our helpful friend from across the street."

"It is nice to meet a good neighbor." Nathan shook hands with Arthur, "If you ever need a lawyer, call me. I am setting up my practice over a few blocks."

"Deed I will."

Clamoring children across the street interrupted them. Lost in thought on the way home from work, Nathan nearly stumbled over his neighbor's children playing on the sidewalk. The littlest one remarked, "That man has no body color."

"Don't worry, he is not sick. All white folks look like that. Papa says he is the new lawyer what lives at the Dykes' house," answered an older sibling.

Swedes, Sven Johnson and his sister Hulda lived on one side of the Dykes. On the other side lived the De Vries, whose grown children had married and moved to the suburbs. Next to them lived Dr. and Mrs. White. Beyond them, a young couple moved into the old Dykstra place. Across the street lived a couple of young black families and beyond them, vacant lots. Nathan felt no racial prejudice. A larger cause consumed him, "justice"—or it was revenge?

In this neighborhood, stubborn older residents desired to spend their remaining years in their own homes. Their children, brought up with strong moral values, helped their parents keep up with their homes and retain their dignity. Saturday mornings, young people filled the neighborhood, washed cars in driveways, mowed lawns, painted trim on houses, occasionally prepared backyard cookouts and ran errands.

Sunday mornings, everyone awoke to peace and quiet. People dutifully spent their morning in worship at the old stone church down the street. Nathan declined Mrs. Dyke's invitation to attend church with them. "I used to attend with my grandparents when I was young. Lately, I have had other priorities."

Afternoons, found the elderly residents of the neighborhood in rocking chairs on their front porches. Hard work all their lives led to hearty approval of their strict religious rules of "no Sunday work."

Nathan found an empty store building a couple of blocks from his apartment. It was an ideal place for his new office. Nathan's office consisted of reference books and files along one wall. He hoped to fill these files with client's cases. Diplomas graced his walls and furniture consisted of an old walnut desk and a couple of chairs. The outer office also showed his lack of decorating skills. It held only the basic necessities—desk, file cabinet, typewriter, reams of paper and chairs for waiting clients.

Chapter Nine

First item of business, Nathan needed to find an efficient secretary. Interviewing young ladies was not a comfortable task he anticipated. His special friend Patty, back home acted more like his big sister. All afternoon, eager young ladies, some talkative, some more taciturn, pushed their résumés before him. All seemed the same by the end of the day. Nathan became weary of the task. As he called "next" the last girl in the outer office, a pert young lady, stepped quickly into his office and set a cup of steaming coffee on his desk.

"For you, sir, fresh from the Corner Café," she said. "I brought cream and sugar if you need it."

"Well, thank you. Black coffee is fine. This smells great," he said, surprised at her candor and pleased at her thoughtfulness in anticipating his needs. Nathan sipped the coffee and nodded in appreciation. "I haven't had a break all afternoon." He paused. "I hope you took time for a cup of coffee yourself."

"Yes. I did. Thank you." Her deep blue eyes that could not fail to hold any man's attention looked directly at him. The lawyer's youthfulness surprised her. She sat back with hands folded in her lap and tried to appear relaxed.

Nathan leaned back in his chair and took a critical look at Sharon Reid's résumé. He studied her seriously before asking a few standard questions. Nathan noted a hint of determination which could be obstinacy if provoked. He admired her composure after such a warm afternoon of waiting. The whole process of selecting a secretary, a necessary component for his success, irritated Nathan. However, his prospect brightened now that he had met Sharon Reid. Short, dark hair curled around her face in sharp contrast to his light complexion. Nathan judged Miss Reid to be about five feet four inches tall. A tailored light blue linen suit flattered her slim figure. "Report to work tomorrow morning at 7:00, Miss Reid," he informed her, rising slowly from his chair.

"Thank you, Mr. Van Veer. You are an answer to my prayers." She tried to return his smile. His large, gentle hand grasped her small, capable one and his eyes looked deep into her own. But, a shudder ran through her at remembering her former fiancé's parting words. "No one wants to marry a cold fish."

Sharon barely heard Mr. Van Veer's next words. "I promise to have our own coffee pot here tomorrow."

"Good, and collect some magazines for your waiting clients. "She ducked her head and quickly exited the room.

"Well, the nerve of her," he thought. Nathan admired her observation and spunk. "She is as spunky as Patty. We should get along fine. I hope Mrs. Dyke has some old magazines.

The smell of fresh coffee greeted Sharon as she arrived at the office the next morning. Over a cup of coffee, Nathan explained more procedures and expectations. Nathan did not want Sharon to think he was a novice, so explained, "I just left the firm of Van De and Van Dann." Though, why should he care what she thought of him?

"It is a very reputable firm. Perhaps one day your reputation will be equal to theirs and I shall have the distinction of being your first secretary." Sharon's broken engagement during her studies at business college left her wary of men. Recently, she had stayed at home and cared for her ailing mother until her death. Now, she could hide no longer. So she applied for the first job the employment agency offered her as secretary to Mr. Van Veer.

Readying the office consumed more time than they anticipated. A few clients who depended on Nathan when he worked with the Van D's continued their loyalty to him. Sharon consulted the appointment book and made arrangements. The confident tone of Nathan's voice in the other room, diplomatic, yet decisive, made her glad he had chosen her over all the other girls.

"Thank you, God." Sharon breathed a prayer of thankfulness that she had found employment. She readied herself for a new challenge by filing away thoughts of the past as she filed folders.

Chapter Ten

Shortly after Nathan opened his office for business, Cynthia Van De arrived at his office desiring to see him. So Sharon announced, "A Miss Cynthia Van De to see you, but she has no appointment. Will you see her?"

"Send her in," said Nathan. Cynthia entered Nathan's office leisurely. She took a good look at his secretary as she passed.

"I am surprised at you, Nate. I thought you did not like beautiful women?" She bent over him and kissed him playfully.

"Don't you like my secretary?" he asked, amused at Cynthia.

"Forget her. I am here now."

"So it seems. Did Daddy send you?" He regretted his disrespect at once. "It is almost lunchtime. Will you have lunch with me?"

"I was hoping you would ask. I am starving, let's go," she said, grateful he agreed to see her.

Nathan took Cynthia's elbows and gently guided her toward the door, giving Sharon a smile and nod as they passed. Why he wanted to irritate her, he did not know. What right did he have to aspire to a wonderful girl like Sharon? The idea beat a persistent refrain in his mind.

Cynthia chattered gaily until she realized her escort's attention lay elsewhere. She was not used to being neglected. Nathan faced her resentfully across the table. Why should a girl be so attractive? She smiled coyly, noticing his gaze. She knew her beauty affected a power over him. "Nathan," she said.

"Hmm-mm," he replied.

"Are you listening?" she inquired tartly. It piqued her to find him so unresponsive. He nodded.

"Have you reconsidered coming back to the firm?" Cynthia thought of Miss Reid working closely with Nathan and jealousy increased her earnestness. "I did not see any clients clamoring for your services this morning."

"Are you calling me a failure?" He was offended at her insinuations.

"No, I am not. You know me better than that, Nathan." His defensive attitude startled her.

"I have enough clients to keep me from starving." He would not let Cynthia sabotage his work.

"Please forgive me, Nathan." He accepted with a shrug.

"You see, Father really needs you now. He hasn't been well lately."

"Why didn't you say so in the first place?" Nathan felt a genuine concern for his former employer. Now, he understood. Cynthia depended on her father not only for his prestige, but emotional support.

"If your father is ill, I will visit him. But, I will not leave my own practice when I am just getting established." He admitted to himself the prestigious advantage of association with the Van D's firm. But, other matters claimed his attention now.

Talk of former acquaintances filled the rest of lunch hour. Cynthia possessed her share of admirers, but she wanted Nathan. Relief settled over him when he waved good-bye to her taxi.

Nathan returned to his office, whistling. Miss Reid stood with her back to him at the file cabinet. Nathan deliberately brushed against her arm as he passed directly to his office without speaking. He wished he knew Sharon better. She radiated a quality of character that Nathan had not known in other women his age. But right now he had committed himself to a cause and he would see it through. Sharon did not approve Nathan's flirtatious behavior, but her heart raved at his nearness. She must keep her emotion under control. She knew that Mr. Van Veer—she dared not think of him as Nathan— did not share her religious values. Her head acknowledged her values, but sometimes she questioned them. For now, she determined to prove herself an efficient secretary to Mr. Van Veer. She could not hope for more.

Chapter Eleven

Robert Reid teased his sister. "I thought that young lawyer might work you too hard and I would have to fix my own dinner."

"So, that is how serious you take me. You are spoiled." Sharon laughed then sobered. "I miss Mother and her savory cooking, too. Mr. Van Veer keeps me busy, but I plan to shoulder my responsibility here at home."

"I have no doubt about that, Sis. I will help with the housework, but cooking skills escape me." Both laughed, remembering his former attempts at cooking—everything was scorched.

"Perhaps, Robert, if you picked me up after work on evening that we have church activities, I would get home earlier than if I took the bus. When father returns from visiting relatives out west, he will gladly help me out in the kitchen," suggested Sharon.

"That is fine with me. By the way, dinner smells tantalizing. I could eat a bear," said Robert.

"Just be glad you don't have to," said his sister.

Sharon hummed a hymn as she dished up their dinner. It had been a while since she felt like singing. She had gladly cared for her mother in her illness. Mother's faith in God never wavered in her pain. Sharon's new job demanded a lot from her, but she faced the challenge willingly. A handsome employer added a motivational bonus. Streetlights came on and Sharon pulled her mother's afghan around her shoulders for comfort. Robert broke her reverie. "Would you like to read the *Press*?" He offered her the evening paper.

"Not tonight. I listened to the news on the radio while I finished the dishes. I will rest here in Mother's chair a few minutes. Then, I must get my clothes ready for work tomorrow."

"So, you are trying to make a good impression on that young lawyer?" Her brother grinned at her.

"No. I am just trying to do a good job. It has been a while since I have worked in an office."

"I'm sorry. I do appreciate that you took time to take care of our mother."

Sharon, full of her own concerns, forgot to ask her brother about his work. "How is the furniture business these days?" she asked.

"David Wagner and I are working on another big order of chairs. He is coming over next Friday evening to challenge me with a game of chess."

"By the way, my boss displays a champion chess trophy on his desk. Perhaps, he might be bribed to give you fellows a few pointers," said Sharon.

"Not a bad idea. Would you mind if I invited him over for supper, too?" asked Robert.

"I suppose not. But, that was not quite what I had in mind." Sharon felt her face flush. She turned so her brother would not notice. Sharon had not planned on cooking for Mr. Van Veer. And, she did not want to appear too eager to get to know him personally. But then, why should she object to her brother having a chess partner over for the evening?

Perhaps, if she were lucky, Mr. Van Veer would appreciate her cooking as much as he did her office skills. She doubted it. A compliment from him was rare. The following day, Mr. Van Veer came from his office and stopped in surprise to see his secretary, Miss Reid, about to leave with a young man. He did not know that she was dating anyone. Then again, he had not inquired into her personal life. Nor had he any intention of doing so.

"Hello, you must be the highly recommended lawyer, Mr. Van Veer. I am pleased to make your acquaintance. My name is Robert Reid."

How stupid of me, thought Nathan. *Sharon did mention a brother.* He reached out his hand and grasped the hand extended to him and looked into eyes the same deep blue as his secretary's. He liked this fellow at once. "It is a mutual pleasure," he agreed.

"I would like to extend a dinner invitation and challenge you to a chess game," said Robert pointing to the trophy on his desk. "My friend David and I could use some pointers. He will be present also. Sharon has agreed to cook dinner for us."

Nathan glanced at Sharon and his lips twitched in a half grin. "In that case, I shall be obliged to accept."

Chapter Twelve

Nathan wondered if David was really a special friend of Robert or Sharon. He added, "Once in a while Mrs. Dyke brings me a casserole or invites me to supper when her daughter Ellen is home for the weekend." He would show Sharon he also had friends. Secretly, he wondered if Sharon's efficiency in the kitchen matched that in the office. No doubt it did.

At the Reid home, Nathan was introduced to Sharon's friend Anne Stone, blond, quiet and easy to look at. She smiled and held out her hand. "It is nice to meet you."

"Likewise, I am sure," Nathan answered.

Another member of the family, their father Frank Reid, was also introduced. A tall, slim man with graying hair and deep blue eyes shook hands with Nathan. A stab of jealousy to have a father ripped through Nathan. "Welcome to our home, Mr. Van Veer. If you young fellows want to get a game of chess set up, I will give the young ladies a hand in the kitchen," said Frank.

The friendliness of these people was unbelievable. Nathan glanced around the room and noticed several religious pictures. David Wagner arrived and introductions were given. Soon afterwards, Sharon announced, "Dinner is ready." Nathan noticed her blushing face and thought it becoming. Her eyes were even bluer. Now, he wondered if the blush resulted from the heat of the kitchen of David's, or his own presence.

"Saved by the bell," Robert said. "David and I will need to brush up on our chess techniques, if we expect to stay in the running for champion chess player with Nathan around."

"You are holding your line of defense quite well. I do not have checkmate yet," answered Nathan.

Mr. Reid sat at the head of the table and Nathan on his right. Anne sat next to Nathan with David on her left at the end of the table. Sharon played it safe and sat between her father and brother. Nathan smiled to himself. The others bowed their heads and Nathan followed while Mr. Reid thanked God for food and friends. Conversation flowed around Nathan, who was lost in his own thoughts. Finally, remembering his manners, he said, "This is a delicious meal, Sharon."

"I agree," said David.

"I told you Sharon is a good cook," boasted Robert, giving his sister a sly smile. Sharon's face reddened again.

"Father and Anne helped," she confessed.

"I never knew my father." Nathan made a grimace. He had not intended to reveal so much of himself.

"I am sorry, Nathan," said Robert.

"I have a father," said David, "but he was not always around when I needed him. It makes me truly appreciate God my Heavenly Father who is always with me."

"Consider us all your friends, Nathan," said Robert. Nathan nodded acknowledgement.

Sharon kept her eyes on her plate, so as not to look directly at Nathan. She could not imagine never knowing her father. Robert moaned and changed the subject. "This delicious meal has dulled my senses. I am not sure I can concentrate on that chess game. What do you think, Nathan?"

"First we ought to help the girls clear the table."

"That is not necessary, Mr. Van Veer," said Sharon. Working for him and having him as a guest in their home presented different situations.

"You cooked the meal. It is only fair that we fellows at least carry the empty dishes back to the kitchen." They all followed Nathan's suggestion and headed for the kitchen, hands full of dishes.

Sharon stood aside to let them pass. When they left the kitchen, Nathan lingered behind with Sharon. "Miss Reid, you may call me Nathan out of the office, if I may call you Sharon."

"Of course, if you insist," she answered.

"I insist. I am sorry to leave you with all this." He gestured toward the dirty dishes. "But, if I do not get back in there, those fellows may disturb my game." He doubted seriously that they would touch his game. He gave Sharon a friendly pat on the shoulder and said, "Don't work too hard, Sharon."

"May I take you home?" David asked Anne. She readily agreed and went to get her jacket. Nathan was secretly happy to find that David was not seeking Sharon's affection.

Many other evenings found Nathan at the Reid home playing chess with Robert. In the game of chess, Nathan remained more control of his life rather than being a victim of circumstances.

But, he was still unable to decipher or unwilling to admit whether the attraction to the Reid home was Sharon, the game of chess or the comfortable feeling of a family who loved God as did his grandparents.

During one furious game of chess, Nathan called, "Checkmate. I finally got you, you blankity-blank." Robert's astonishment was not so much that he lost, but Nathan's reaction in winning.

"Sorry," mumbled Nathan. "I was engrossed in one of my cases. Chess helps my concentration."

Robert laughed good-naturedly. "I thought you were angry with me for giving you a hard time. You sure act like you are in real combat."

"Maybe I am," Nathan said softly and began gathering up his knights and carefully placing them in their cases.

"Anything I can help you with, friend?" Robert asked.

"No, I must do this myself."

"You work too hard," said Robert. "What do you think of going out to City Park on Saturday? We will ask Sharon to fix us a picnic and accompany us. We can relax in the warm sun one more time before cold weather settles in for good."

Nathan thought of declining until the mention of Sharon's name. "I have not been on a picnic in ages." He hesitated. "I am not sure if I should take time off from my research, and as you may have noticed, I am not much of a conversationalist unless you count debate in court."

"We can talk to the birds and squirrels, if you like," suggested Robert.

"That should be safe enough," Nathan answered. A day in the park with Sharon might prove most pleasant, he thought.

Saturday morning the sun shone just warm enough to be comfortable with a light sweater. A slight breeze stirred the leaves of maple trees. "I like these grand old maple trees," said Sharon as they parked their picnic basket on a blanket beneath one.

"These trees are like the ones on Grandfather's place along the Thornapple River," said Nathan, glad for Sharon's appreciation of the trees. Nathan looked up at the trees where patches of sky shone through. Just then a squirrel dropped a nutshell down on Nathan that he had gathered from a neighboring oak.

"It looks like this squirrel wants to join the conversation. What did I tell you about talking to the squirrels?" said Robert.

They both laughed. It was the first time Sharon had heard him laugh. His whole face lit up.

Sharon's mind was filled with questions, but for the moment she was happy to see Nathan relax. She wondered about his home and grandfather. Did they take long comfortable walks along the river? Sharon glanced at Nathan and their eyes met. He smiled and she quickly looked away.

Later that evening, Robert and Nathan relaxed on the front porch of the Reid home. Robert leaned against the rail as he sat on the top step. Nathan sat on the rail above him, one leg swinging. "You are a lucky man, Robert. You have a sister and a father. Patty, granddaughter of my friend Dr. Perkins, is the closest I have to a sister."

"I heard you mention a mother and grandparents. I have neither," said Robert. "I do not consider it luck, one way or the other. I prefer to think of it as God's providence. He knows us and gives us what is best for each of us, though we may not understand. Also, sometimes, men mess up God's plan."

"I agree with that," Nathan replied heatedly.

David and Anne strolled by holding hands. "Come on up, friends," called Robert. "Sharon, we have company."

Anne and David looked at each other with a special smile. "You might as well be the first to know," said David. "I have asked Anne to be my wife, and she said yes."

"Congratulations." Robert and Nathan shook David's hand. Sharon embraced Anne.

"Oh, Anne, that is wonderful."

Nathan wondered how it would feel to have Sharon look at him like Anne looked at David.

"This calls for a celebration," said Robert. "Come on inside. We have some cold lemonade and some Sharon's chocolate cake."

Chapter Thirteen

Nathan turned his Chevy car east out of the city toward the rolling hills and tree-lined roads that led home. He had forgotten how peaceful a drive through the country could be after living in the noisy city. Little farms dotted the scene. Bare trees waited for warm blanket of snow. A new freeway crept toward his village. The remembrance of other Thanksgivings filled Nathan with ecstasy. Some years, the first big snow fell on Thanksgiving. Neighborhood children gathered on Page Hill with their sleds. When they tired of sledding, they made tracks and began a game of fox and geese. Other years, snow arrived as early as Halloween and by Thanksgiving the ice on Hunter's Pond froze solid enough to hold skaters. He and Patty spent many hours wearing off a big Thanksgiving or Christmas dinner in this manner.

Great-Aunt Hettie, Grandfather's sister, always shared Thanksgiving with the family. She made her presence felt from the first moments of her arrival. Forthwith, she proceeded to fortify every one with friendly laughter and firm hugs from her sturdy frame.

Hettie's husband, tall, frail Uncle Pete, followed quietly behind her, smiling and greeting everyone with a handshake.

He said little, but his eyes followed Aunt Hettie. His lop-sided smile provided evidence of his adoration.

One day, Uncle Pete quietly passed away with a heart attack. Nathan assumed that the poor man's heart was overwhelmed by his wife's vivaciousness and could no longer stand the strain.

Perhaps, Nathan inherited his talent for debate and energy to see right justified from his aunt. The day he passed his bar exams, she rejoiced with him, proud of her grandnephew's achievements. Lost in thought, Nathan almost missed the turnoff to grandfather's place. His car heater failed to produce much heat and Nathan arrived home chilled to the bone.

Mary, Nathan's mother, watched from the front window as eager as a young child. She wore a bright flowered blouse and a skirt that Patty and Nathan picked out for her. As he swung open the door, she met him with a hug. "Hi, Jonny, how is the big city?"

"Busy and noisy, more people than a county fair," he answered. A cat purred against his leg. Nathan reached down and stroked the cat's arched back.

"Tabby is hungry," said Mary. She picked him up and held him against her cheek.

"Come on in," Aunt Hettie called. "That wind feels like winter is coming." Nathan hugged her and both hearts were warmed.

He kissed his grandmother on the cheek as she stirred the gravy. "Welcome home, Son," she greeted him. Grandmother still moved quickly, but somewhat stiffly. She wore her long hair braided around her head. Her long skirts were more modest than fashion.

Grandfather stood warming his back by the wood heater in the living room and observed his family. "Your fire still chases the chill away," commented Nathan as they shook hands.

"That is the final function of your old apple tree," Grandfather replied.

"Patty and I spent many summer hours in the branches of that tree observing the town and exchanging confidences. I will miss that tree, even if I am too old to climb trees anymore."

Nathan noticed his grandfather's stooped shoulders and balding head. Only a gray rim of hair remained. His glasses perched on his bulbous nose beneath bushy eyebrows and wrinkled forehead. But his cheerful smile remained the same. "It is good to be home," said Nathan with a catch in his voice.

"Hurry and get washed up." His mother scolded him like a little boy. "We have been cooking all morning and everything is ready." The old Kalamazoo wood cook-stove warmed the whole kitchen and reddened the ladies' faces.

"I brought my special cranberry salad," commented Aunt Hettie, making a place for it on the crowded table. Nathan took his place between his mother and grandfather. All bowed their heads and Grandfather offered a sincere prayer of thanks and did not forget to thank God for bringing Jonathan home to them again. Nathan's heart welled up at the tenderness of the old man whom he loved. The next hour, good food, laughter and pleasant memories of times past prevailed.

"We made your favorite pie, Jonny. I peeled the apples," Mary announced proudly.

"A delicious ending for a wonderful meal," Nathan sighed. "Even Tabby is begging for a handout." He slipped the grateful cat a morsel under the table.

"I have just the remedy for a full stomach," said Grandfather. "A little exercise is what we need. Come out to the shop with me, Jonathan. Let the ladies cope with the dishes." Nathan gave a nod of satisfaction.

Grandfather handed Nathan a piece of sandpaper as they entered the orderly workshop. "What do you think of my latest project? It is for your grandmother's Christmas. Her old table has served long enough. I promised her a new table someday. I plan to surprise her at Christmas."

Together they sanded and reminisced in a comfortable atmosphere of companionship. "Grandfather," Nathan began, "you know I love you. So, I hope you understand when I say, I need to find my father. I have thought about it for a long time. However, I admit my motives are not pure love. Yet, other times I need him as a father."

"Do not waste time on hatred, Son." Grandfather had a thousand proverbs in his head. "If your parents hadn't gotten together, you would not be here. A good opinion of one's self makes a man courageous and well balanced. But, a low opinion makes a man fearful and lost."

Nathan considered this. Aloud he said, "I wonder what characteristics besides anger I inherited from my father."

"Your father and his parents before him proved themselves good neighbors many times. He made one mistake and I am convinced he has suffered guilt every day since. It took me a long time to forgive him. But, once I held you, I started to forgive him. You grew into a fine lad and I almost thanked him for giving such a grandson. You make us proud. Hatred flows against everything. Try to let God's love replace your anger. In the final plan, everyone is responsible for his or her own actions.

"As for inherited qualities, one can never tell. Throughout life, you may discover positive hidden talents that will surprise you. Develop them and thank God," admonished Grandfather. "Someday, you will need to care for your mother. She will not understand your hate. She knows only love."

"I appreciate your care of Mother, Grandfather. I assure you I will provide for her. You know I have always loved her."

"That you have, Son." They worked awhile. Grandfather broke the silence. "How are things at the office and the courtroom?"

"I enjoy representing people who cannot help themselves. This makes up for the injustice done to my mother."

Grandfather listened and finally understood the boy's choice of a career as a lawyer when he seemed so talented in working with his hands. The old man wondered if dealing with family court might not be a cruel twist of fate for Jonathan, causing his own pain to overwhelm him. Instead, he asked, "How is your new secretary? Is she as nice as Patty?"

"Patty and I will always be friends. Miss Reid is a very energetic, efficient secretary. She is very helpful and kind to my clients and me. I really admire her." He did not tell his grandfather how much.

"Miss Reid's brother is a worthy adversary in a chess game. He has invited me to their home. You would like them, Grandfather. Their belief in God is as strong as yours."

Thank you, God. Grandfather sent a prayer heavenward, grateful that his grandson chose his friends wisely. The name Reid caused Grandfather to wonder if they were connected to Suzanne Reid, with whom Jonathan's father had been engaged.

Jonathan continued, "Miss Reid, Sharon, cared for her mother during a long illness. After her mother died, Sharon came to work for me."

"I am glad you have such good friends," said Grandfather. "But, I am getting tired. Shall we finish this tomorrow? We'll see if we can get a cup of coffee. There should be a fresh pot by now."

They had just poured their coffee when Patty knocked at the door, "Hi Mary. Are you ready to begin that new afghan today?" Patty taught Mary to crochet by starting the first few rows for her. Over the years Mary made several nice afghans. Once they accumulated, she gave them to Patty to donate to her grandfather's patients at the nursing home.

Mary went to get her yarn. Patty blew on her hands. "If this cold spells holds, Hunter's pond should be frozen deep enough for skating."

"Bring your skates tomorrow. I will sharpen them after I finish helping Grandfather." Nathan poured a cup of coffee and motioned for Patty to sit at the table.

"This should warm your bones. And, here is something for your sweet tooth." Nathan passed a plate of Grandmother's cookies. "You and Mom have fun with your yarn, but Grandfather and I have some business out in the shop."

Chapter Fourteen

Back in the city, Ellen Dyke celebrated Thanksgiving with her parents. She regretted that Nathan usually managed to be away for a holiday when she came home. Sharon, Robert and Frank Reid spent Thanksgiving Day at the Wagner home with David and Anne and David's father, Mark. After a bountiful feast, the ladies went into the kitchen to survey the dirty dishes and the surprising amount of leftovers.

"I am glad Nathan visited his family over the holiday," Anne said, content with her husband and new baby on the way.

"He does seem to miss his family, especially his mother. He instructed me to order her flowers every Friday," Sharon commented.

"He will make some girl a thoughtful, romantic husband," teased Anne.

Sharon blushed. "He is not hard to like. He is a fair, but demanding employer. But I cannot consider dating a non-Christian." This she said more to convince herself than her friend. She did not mention that she prayed daily for Nathan to accept God's love. He had mentioned that his grandparents were Christians.

A different discussion took place in the other room. "My cup of thanks runs over this year," said David, thinking of his wife and unborn child. "Christ in my life makes this all possible." He spread his hands out to include his home and friends. "Robert, I thank you for your friendship and for rescuing me from lonely hours in a bar."

"We rejoice with you. Now, your child will be born into a Christian home. He will grow up knowing God's love," said Mr. Reid. Frank Reid did not recognize his old friend Mark, formerly Martin, who had changed over the years. Mark listened to the conversation with interest. He also gave no indication of recognition of Frank Reid. Of late, that pain in Mark's chest occurred more frequently. He knew time was running out. His father experienced this kind of pain and suddenly he was gone. How Mark wished his life had been different. Memories flooded back.

"David, there are some things in my life I wish I could change, especially the way I treated you and your mother. I am afraid I have not been a very good father."

"I forgave you, Father, when Jesus forgave me. God will forgive you too, if you sincerely ask him. Would you like to trust God's forgiveness now?"

"Yes," Mark answered with tears in his eyes. "I have seen the difference in your life."

They knelt and David prayed earnestly, "Dear God, help my father to know the joy of forgiveness and the peace of your love."

"Amen," echoed around the room.

Now that Mark had received Christ's love and forgiveness, he longed to find his child and make amends. As he considered how to do this, a pain surged through him like a crushing weight. When he awoke, David stood beside him. "You are in St. Mary's Hospital. You gave us quite a scare."

Mark reached out a hand and smiled, "God is with me."

Mark made a slow recovery from his heart attack. But today, he was in good spirits. David and Anne invited him to visit his grandson Mark, named in his honor. Mark was honored as he watched the child, but how could he tell his son that he only assumed the name Mark so many years ago?

The warmth of little Mark in his arms brought back old memories of the day he first held David, and anguish over another child he never held. "Thank God for forgiveness."

"David, you saved yourself much heartache by finding God before you became a father. Your son will know a father's love filled with the Heavenly Father's love, a wonderful combination."

David put his arm around his father's shoulder. "I love you." The doorbell rang before he could say more. David hurried to answer it. Voices of friends sounded in the hallway.

"We want to meet the new baby," said Sharon. "Nathan arrived just as we were leaving, so we persuade him to come along."

"Congratulations." Robert and Nathan shook David's hands.

As the fellows shook hands, Anne took the baby from her father-in-law and held him for Sharon's inspection. "He is perfect." Sharon caressed the baby's blond fuzzy head.

"Nathan, I want you to meet my father, Mark I," said David.

Nathan's attention was drawn from Sharon holding the baby to the man being introduced. They stared at each other a moment before Mark spoke. "It is a small world. Mr. Wagner and I met some time ago when he worked for the Van D's.

"That is right. I own my own practice now," said Nathan.

"I am not surprised. You were an intense young lawyer."

After a short visit, the friends prepared to leave. Nathan felt a jab of jealousy thinking of David and Robert with their fathers and David with Little Mark. Though he did not understand why he felt thus when fathers symbolized his anger.

Chapter Fifteen

llen Dyke was aware of Nathan's presence in the house when she visited her parents, observed his routine of leaving the house early and arriving late in the evening. If he came home early he carried a briefcase of work. Even on Saturday he often returned to his office for easy access to his reference books. Sundays, he allowed himself the luxury of sleeping late. Occasionally, Ellen persuaded her mother to invite Nathan to dinner on a Friday evening.

Nathan spread his books on the dining table, which also served as his desk. "Come in," he called in answer to a knock at the door.

"Please come to dinner this evening. Ellen is home and you need a break," said Mrs. Dyke.

"Perhaps I do. I have been pushing myself lately." Nathan did not object to Mrs. Dyke's motherly attention. His grandmother always fussed over him. However, on several occasions he declined Mrs. Dyke's offer.

Ellen and Nathan conversed with ease. Mr. and Mrs. Dyke listened, adding a comment now and then. Ellen talked of her pupils and she asked Nathan about his work. "You know a lawyer must keep his clients' confidence," he reminded her.

This also meant he did not wish to talk about himself. So, they talked of college days and events of the times. Ellen felt a certain possessiveness of Nathan, but he refused to be tied to anyone's beck and call. Ellen was good company. She did not possess Cynthia's charm and poise, nor did she mystify him as Sharon.

Nathan knew that Sharon disapproved of his association with Cynthia. He noted her reactions during her brief announcements of his appointments the day Cynthia came to his office. But, Sharon's efficiency in the office and at her home left little room for criticism. Nathan wished that he had certain matters settled about his father. Then he would be free to pursue a relationship with a nice girl, perhaps even Sharon. Nathan thought of the relationship of his grandparents, how they loved each other.

Invitations arrived at Nathan's office for a special Christmas party at the City Hotel. It was from Van De and Van Dann's law firm.

"I wish I did not have to invite Nathan's secretary," Cynthia complained to her father. She noticed how Sharon eyed her when she visited Nathan's office.

"No need to worry, Cynthia dear. You know your power over him." Cynthia smiled. Yes, she knew. "Besides," her father continued, "if the party is in honor of Nathan's new office you cannot very well neglect his secretary."

Robert, Nathan's chess partner, also received an invitation. With Nathan's permission and persuasion, Robert invited Patty Perkins to be his guest.

Nathan sat on the edge of Sharon's desk when she arrived at work, obviously waiting to speak with her. "I want to talk to you about the invitation that arrived yesterday," he said. "I hope you do not mind if I do not invite you as my guest. Van De and Dann would not consider it proper for me to escort my secretary to such an affair as their Christmas party."

"Why should I mind? You are free to escort whomever you please." Though she wondered why he bothered to mention it. Did he really want her to go?

"Since the invitation came here to the office, you are also invited. You may also invite anyone."

"You flatter yourself to think I mind," she retorted.

"Your brother spoke to me, about you."

"I cannot imagine about what." She tried not to show her surprise or irritation.

"He said I might not fit your categorization of an ideal man. He also told me about your broken engagement. The man must have been an idiot to not want to marry you."

"How dare Robert?" Sharon's face reddened, not only that Nathan should know of her rejection, but at the hint of his interest in her. "I am perfectly capable of managing my own affairs."

"Oh, you are, are you? You mean by dodging the issue. Perhaps someday you will consider going out on a date with me?"

"Would that be wise, since we work together?"

Nathan shrugged. "You are important to me; I would not like to lose a good secretary."

Nathan started for his own office door. "In case you are interested I am taking Ellen Dyke." Of course, she was interested. But, she would never let him know. No other girl intrigued Nathan as Sharon. She could cheer his heart like sunshine after a rain. But, after Robert's warning that she only dated men she considered Christian, Nathan decided to bide his time. He hardly fit her classification of Christian, but he did not consider himself a heathen. True, it had been a while since he had talked to God or gone to church.

Nathan knew when he invited Ellen Dyke to accompany him that Cynthia also, would be aggravated with him. Cynthia expected him to escort her. Nathan went with Robert to meet

Patty at the Greyhound bus station the evening before the party. Patty spent the night with Ellen. Petite Patty and tall Ellen, a contrasting pair, became good friends. They shared a common interest in their admiration of Nathan, yet each envious of the position of the other in his life.

Sharon felt a little uncomfortable at the thought of attending a party given by the Van D's. But her brother lent his moral support, so she invited Paul De Witt from her church as her escort.

Ellen, elegant in a red sheath dress and high heels, matched Nathan's height, making them an outstanding couple. Nathan rented a tuxedo for the evening and advised Robert to do the same.

Nathan nodded approval of Sharon's new attire, a light blue wool suit and hat to match the color of her eyes. He also took note of her date, a tall, dark, attractive young man. This caused him to ponder seriously if he would ever stand a chance with Sharon.

Mr. Van De stood by Cynthia's side as guests entered the reception. Cynthia had coaxed her father to prepare a celebration in honor of Nathan's new law practice, under the guise of a Christmas party, knowing Nathan would never consent if he knew the party was in his honor.

Now, Cynthia questioned her wisdom in planning such a party when she observed Nathan with Ellen. Cynthia, convinced that Sharon would be Nathan's date, had planned how she would lure Nathan away from her. When the crowd shifted and Cynthia got a chance she hurried to greet them. She talked out of nervous compulsion and put on her upper-class voice. She managed to make the most trivial things seem exciting.

Now that the guest of honor had arrived, Cynthia hurried to her father's side. Mr. Van De, sixty, short and plump, wore a hearing aid behind his right ear and had the beginnings of a double chin.

"Make your toast now, Father," Cynthia coaxed.

Mr. Van De cleared his throat for attention. "I wish to make a toast to Nathan Van Veer, our former partner. I wish to compliment him and wish him the best in his new law practice. At this time, I wish to present him with this plaque as a token of his former association with the Van D's." Nathan's surprise was genuine. After all, they did not throw a party when he left their firm. Nathan accepted their token of appreciation and promised himself he would discuss the matter with Van De later. One look at Cynthia told him she generated the idea. He was glad he had left the firm. Cynthia and her father suffocated him.

Patty was still getting used to hearing Nathan's surname as Van Veer. All her life she had known him as Nathan Simon. Sharon and Paul moved toward the punch bowl. Sharon wondered if every other woman in the room felt as colorless as she did. She did not wish to see Cynthia fawning over Nathan. Paul considered his good fortune to be Sharon's date for the evening, unaware that her interest in Nathan was more than professional. Sharon and Paul left the party, walked along Monroe Avenue admiring the animated Christmas displays in store windows, and shared a quite dinner before hailing a cab home.

Cynthia took Nathan by the arm, "Come, Nathan dear. I want you to meet some people." And she whisked him away to meet some of her father's friends. They talked to a succession of familiar half-known people seen once or twice a year. Robert and Patty rescued Ellen, who had been left standing by herself. Robert took Ellen and Patty by an arm and followed right behind Nathan and Cynthia He introduced the girls and himself as Cynthia introduced Nathan. Nathan, taking the cue from Robert, took Ellen's arm. "This is my date, Ellen Dyke," he said.

After a few more brief introductions, Cynthia gave up. "There is someone I need to speak with," she said and made a hasty exit. Her determined happiness increased thereafter with her liquor intake.

Nathan and Robert made their excuses to Mr. Van De and Van Dann and left. Cynthia considered the party a flop and the entire evening ruined. Oh, her caterers outdid themselves, but her failure with Nathan left her miserable. Mr. Van De liked Nathan and greeted his friends heartily, amused that Nathan outwitted Cynthia.

Mr. Van De had gone along with Cynthia planning for the party. He could not deny her anything. He also admired Nathan's independent spirit and secretly hoped that someday he would succumb to Cynthia's persuasion.

Chapter Sixteen

Sharon awoke with a start and shut off her alarm. She rejoiced that last night she nearly finished her Christmas shopping. She purchased a new harmonica for her father and a new sweater for Robert. In the past, Mother had knit him a new sweater each Christmas. Sharon purchased gloves for David and a china bell for Anne's collection. She still wanted to get a small gift for Nathan, but was undecided. Perhaps she and Anne would take a trip out of the new mall. Next week, she planned to bake for the elderly at church.

Sharon enjoyed the excitement of shopping downtown. Children and adults blocked the sidewalks as they watched store window displays in action. She thrilled at the sound of Christmas carols and the ringing of Salvation Army bells. Foggy clouds of exhaust followed busses as they roared up to the corner where weary shoppers waited to go home.

The next morning, Sharon fixed a quick breakfast of toast and coffee and hurried to catch a bus. Robert had left earlier. Usually, Sharon waited alone at her bus stop, but she saw a movement at the edge of her vision and turned her head. She noticed a man hunched up against the cold morning air. Sharon shivered, not so much from the cold, but a premonition. An ordinary day became a nightmare. Sharon glanced up the street and hoped for more traffic at this early hour. Lights shone in only a few houses. Sharon held her token ready. Relief engulfed her when she spied the bus approaching. But, at the moment the young man shoved her so she stumbled in the snow. He grabbed her purse and ran disappearing behind the houses.

The bus driver observed what had happened. But he was helpless to do anything to help Sharon except to radio police headquarters and report the incident. Sharon still clutched her token as she brushed snow off herself. She assured the bus driver she was not hurt, only shaken and robbed.

Sharon arrived at work lacking her usual confident stride. There was a glint of tears in her eyes as she ducked her head and hung up her coat.

Nathan observed her distress and put a sheltering arm around her shivering shoulders. "Come into my office." Sharon meekly went with him and dropped down into the chair across from Nathan's desk. She accepted the steaming cup of coffee he offered her, but she could not stop shivering.

"What happened to upset you so?" he inquired.

Sharon related the events of the morning. Nathan was infuriated that someone should try to harm Sharon. He reached for her hand and pulled her up to him. She did not draw away when he put his arms around her. Sharon felt his breath on her hair and drew comfort from the fact he cared for her. In his mind, Nathan saw the man who assaulted his mother. He drew in a sharp breath.

"Nathan, what is it?" she asked, lifting her face to his.

"I am so glad you are all right." He kissed her lightly on the forehead. "Take the day off. I will call your brother, or if you prefer, I will take you home."

"Really, I think I should earn my wages today. After all, I was just robbed." She managed a weak smile. Sharon's purse was found several blocks from the bus stop. She appreciated the return of the purse, as it had been a gift from her mother. But purse-snatchers were difficult to apprehend. The approaching Christmas season made thieves desperate for cash. This one did not fare so well. Sharon had spent most of her cash on her shopping the evening before.

Nathan kept a close watch on Sharon the rest of the day. She amazed him. After a cup of coffee and a few extra minutes to get composed, she went about the day's duties with more poise and calm than Nathan felt. He could not bear to think of anything happening to Sharon. She told him, "God's hand of protection kept me safe."

Nathan admitted to himself the depth of his feelings for Sharon were more than the sister of his good friend and more than a secretary to him, but for now, he must be content with the memory of the beating of her heart against his chest.

Even though Sharon was very tired, she found it difficult to fall asleep that night. "Think about something pleasant," she told herself. She smiled wryly. She would think of Nathan and his arms around her.

Robert suggested to Nathan, "If it will not inconvenience you too much, I would appreciate it if you could give my sister a ride to work, at least until after the holidays. Sharon has agreed to this, if you are willing."

"Willing? It would be a pleasure. It is no inconvenience," he relayed to Robert. Previous visits to the Reid home were at Robert's invitation to play chess. Now, he had Sharon's consent. Sharon thought it ridiculous to still feel so jittery, but she went about handling her office duties with confidence.

I know that I do not measure up to Sharon's ideal of a special man, Nathan thought. *I wish I had her strong faith. Then maybe I could forgive my father. I smoke a pipe in the courtroom. It adds a stern effect to my lawyer image. I drink socially, when the occasion calls for it, and I have not attended church in some time. But, I have high morals and my grandparents taught me about God. Sharon is a very special girl and I can dream and hope. I know my grandparents would approve of her, but how to get Sharon approve of me*, he wondered. *I will send her a bouquet tomorrow as a start.*

Sharon was pleased when the bouquet of flowers was delivered to her desk.

Nathan's spirits were lifted when a few days later, Sharon suggested, "Would you like to go Christmas caroling with a group from our church? Robert and I are going."

"I never participated in this kind of event before, but remember carolers singing for my grandparents. I would be glad to join you and Robert."

Robert shared a songbook with Nathan while Sharon seemed occupied with Paul, much to Nathan's dismay. The stars were out and the cool evening air exhilarating. They sang to several shut-ins, then went to the Christian Home and sang to senior residents there, before returning to Paul's home for hot chocolate and cookies. Laughter filled the house.

Paul, busy serving hot chocolate, left Sharon sitting near the Christmas tree. Nathan saw his chance and came up behind her and spoke. Startled, Sharon jumped. "You need not act like a frightened colt, just because I wanted to talk to you. This is a nice party."

Sharon's hands trembled, and she spilled chocolate on her skirt. "Now look what you made me do." He offered her his napkin. "I must go and rinse this off." She made her way through the crowd, glad to escape his searching eyes for now. She would have to face him at work soon enough. Sharon could not explain her reactions, only that he made her nervous when he paid her special attention.

"I don't think I can stand another heartbreak, Lord," Sharon prayed.

Chapter Seventeen

C hristmas morning Sharon, Robert and their father sat at the breakfast table, each lost in their own thoughts, this first Christmas without their mother. Attempting to show a merry Christmas spirit, Sharon planned a special breakfast, but it did not seem to be helping.

"Let's open our presents," Sharon said cheerfully, coaxing them to gather around the tree as her mother did in years past.

"A sweater," said Robert. "I had resigned myself to my old one for another year." Robert was pleased and touched by Sharon's thoughtfulness. He slipped it on, a perfect fit. "Thanks, Sis. Now, let's see what you have."

Sharon held up a blue silk blouse from Robert and a watch from her father. "You two did a super job of shopping." She hugged them both.

"Listen." Father put his harmonica to his lips and played a Christmas carol. Robert and Sharon joined in singing. After attending Christmas morning services they visited with David and Anne Wagner.

During the night, it snowed four or five inches. Snowplows had gone through by the time Nathan shaved and showered and drank a cup of coffee. He looked forward to the day at his grandparents'.

Grandmother's surprise and smiles were plenty reward for replacing her old table with the new one, which had been hiding in Grandfather's shop. She set out her best china cups and they enjoyed a leisurely breakfast of bacon, eggs and Grandmother Simon's special coffeecake.

After breakfast, Nathan's mother urged them to open their gifts. "Hurry up, Jonny. I want to see what you got me in that big package under the tree." Folds of bright red spilled out from the paper.

"Oh-h-h," she gasped, "so pretty." A skirt and sweater to match were Nathan's gift to her.

Nathan purchased new boots and jackets for his grandparents. They enjoyed the outdoors and always appreciated practical gifts. His grandparents gave him the usual shirt and tie. And Grandmother baked special goodies for him to take back to the city.

Nathan also received a knitted scarf from Sharon and a jackknife from Robert and a hand-carved nameplate for his desk from the Wagners.

After a satisfy dinner, Grandfather retreated to his shop. Nathan followed. Today, Grandfather felt an urgency to tell Nathan again, "Grandmother and I love you very much, but more than that we want you to know God. The Heavenly Father also loves you. We hope that someday we will all meet in heaven."

Chapter Eighteen

The telephone rang. "Hello, Jonathan, my boy." Dr. Perkins' familiar voice sounded pleasant as he inquired, "How is business?"

Nathan pleased to hear from his old friend had answered, "Fine, sir. I just talked to a couple of new clients." Then, the bolt of lightning struck him.

"I am sorry, Jonathan, to always be the one to bring you bad news. But, I will just come to the point. Your grandparents were in an automobile accident this morning. They did not survive." Nathan could not speak. He could not believe what he just heard.

Thoughts of his last conversation with Grandfather raced through his mind. *We will not always be here. We want you to be with us in heaven.* He remembered his own difficulty in believing the Heavenly Father.

"Jonathan, are you there?" Dr. Perkins' voice sounded insistent. "We have your mother at our house. She was not with them."

"Thank you," he murmured. He did not know exactly for what, but he was grateful his mother was in good hands. "I will come right away." Nathan stalked out of his office. "Cancel my appointments for the next few days. I am needed at home. I will be in touch with you later." Sharon made a move toward him, a gesture of comfort when she saw his ashen face. "Take the week off," he said. A moment later the door slammed shut behind him.

"Help him, Lord," Sharon prayed.

Nathan shivered on the park bench outside his office. Though the sun warmed his back, it could not warm his spirit from the effects of the chilling message he had just received from Dr. Perkins. Shaken to the core, Nathan wondered where he would get strength to go on. His grandparents had always been there for him. They seemed so strong and indestructible. Only a few weeks ago, they celebrated Christmas together. Nathan watched the pigeons for a few minutes. A pigeon pecked Nathan on the foot. Slowly he got up to leave. "Okay, fellow, I am leaving."

Dr. Perkins greeted Nathan with a friendly handshake. "Your mother is waiting for you inside."

"Hi, Jonny," his mother said courageously.

"Hi, Mom." He gave the plump little lady a big hug and kissed her cheek. He wondered what the future held for the two of them.

"Come, Jonathan," said Maggie, the doctor's wife. "Supper is ready. We can talk afterwards."

"Sit by me," coaxed Mary, his mother.

After dinner, they explained to Mary about her parent's death. She did not completely understand, but Patty took her under her wing and involved her in a game of checkers. Nathan and Dr. Perkins talked late into the night. Finally, Dr. Perkins said, "I think this old man better get to bed, if he wants to get up in the morning. Maggie laid out some blankets for you, Nathan, here on the sofa."

Nathan doubted sleep would ever come. Darkness settled down on the room and lent its lonely mood to the heart of Nathan. Finally, exhaustion overcame him and he slept fitfully.

In the morning, he did not feel much rested. Sooner or later, he would have to go to his grandparent's home. But, for now he was content to be in the Perkins' household, cared for by friends.

Maggie stirred in the kitchen and the aroma of fresh coffee reached Nathan. "Good morning, Jonathan. If you wish, I will take Mary shopping for a dress for the funeral. You will be free to make funeral arrangements. Later, you can take her to say good-bye to her parents."

"Would you like me to go with you, today, Nathan?" Patty suggested and poured another cup of coffee for him.

"I would like that." Nathan dreaded going alone and valued Patty's friendship at this moment. He thought of the little things he would miss about his grandparents, all the "never-agains" of life. Grief weighed heavy like a boulder on his chest.

Nathan notified Sharon of his grandparents' passing. "I am so sorry, Nathan. I understand your loss. I will be praying for you. I will be here at the office taking care of any necessary mail and messages if you need me." Sharon informed the Dykes, who sent their condolences along with the Reids and Wagners.

"These flowers arrived from Sharon and Robert and the Wagners," said Patty. Nathan nodded acknowledgement.

Nathan found his task of taking his mother to say good-bye to her parents the most difficult thing he had ever been called upon to do. Mary looked puzzled and did not fully understand. She talked to her parents and fingered the silk linings of the caskets. She patted her father's forehead. "Poor Daddy, got an owie." Nathan turned his face to hide his tears. Mary stood talking to her parents a few more moments. "I got mad at you, Daddy, when you did not come home. I do not want you to go away again. But, Jonny says you have to. Momma, please wake up and talk to me. I guess I will live with Jonny now. I will try to be brave, but I get scared. Patty says she will still be my friend. I love you, Momma and Daddy. But I think I am still a little mad at you for going away."

"Time for the service to start," Nathan muttered.

"Come, dear, your parents worked hard all their lives. Now, they deserve a rest in heaven." Maggie Perkins gently led Mary to a seat.

Mary rocked herself back and forth like one trying to ease an intolerable pain. Nathan's pain and loneliness also seemed intolerable.

"Give me strength, Lord." It had been a long time since Nathan had prayed. He realized suddenly how much he missed talking to God.

Only a small group of people gathered to pay their last respects to a couple who lived among them for many years, yet in reality, were not of them. A few older residents remembered earlier days when John Simon first opened his repair shop and provided needed service to the community.

Young Celia glowed with her pregnancy and joined her friends at church and social gatherings of the town. After the birth of Mary, people of the town shunned her. But Celia courageously held her head up, going about the task of raising her retarded child and later her grandchild. She possessed more strength of character than those who snubbed her, afraid of their own reactions should such circumstances befall them.

After the service, Nathan took his mother for a ride in the country. She leaned back and smiled. He allowed himself to relax a bit too, and forget some of his problems while in her company. A special bond drew Nathan and his mother together. At an early age, he sensed his mother's difference. She opened his eyes to see simple pleasures that other adults passed by in their rush through life. At times, frustration overtook him when he could not reconcile the hatred for his father with the love of his mother.

Two weeks passed before Nathan returned to his office. "It is good to have you back, Nathan. I have laid the most urgent mail and telephone messages on your desk." Sharon brought him coffee as she had on the afternoon they first met. Only today, he looked tired and haggard.

"I have been praying for you." He looked at her, a queer grin twisting the corner of his mouth. He was not sure how he felt about someone talking to God for him. And what was her petition?

Yet Nathan admired Sharon's faith in God. "Perhaps I do need someone to pray for me, now that my grandparents are no longer here to petition God on my behalf."

Nathan reached in his pocket and handed Sharon a piece of paper. "Put this number on my phone list." Sharon could not help noticing his sad expression. She went to her own office and wrote the number down before she forgot. *Christian Home, this must be where Nathan's mother now lives.* Sharon admired Nathan's devotion to his mother. He often called her and sent her little gifts in addition to her weekly bouquet. A pang of loneliness swept over Sharon as she thought of her own mother. Her mother had prayed for her and showed her the way to God. It comforted her to know that they would meet again in heaven. The phone rang, bringing Sharon back to the present. That evening, she and Nathan worked late on the backlog of work.

"I think we have done enough for one day," said Nathan, gathering up his papers. "I will work on some of these at home tonight."

"I can come in earlier tomorrow, if you wish," Sharon suggested.

"It is not necessary. But may I give you a lift home?"

"Yes." Sharon nodded. She felt that the buses were safe enough after the holidays, but she missed their shared rides.

Nathan attempted to carry on a conversation. "How are your brother and father?"

"They are fine and missing you." She paused. "How are you doing, Nathan? It may help you to talk about your losses, bring your burden out into the open where it can be looked at and shared. When my mother died, we all walked around each other, lost in our own thoughts. Finally, our pastor got us to talk out our feelings to each other. We all missed Mother so, each in our own way. But we received comfort as we shared our grief. Agony seems socially unacceptable as if we are not supposed to weep, but grief leaves an unremitting ache."

Nathan shrugged. "What can I say? I depended too deeply on them."

Chapter Nineteen

"I should be comforting Mother, but I can find no comfort for myself," Nathan sighed.

"Would you mind if I visited your mother?" Sharon suggested.

"You would do that?" Nathan asked in surprise.

"I know how difficult it is to lose a parent. If I cannot comfort your mother I can at least visit her. I will pray for your peace of mind also."

Nathan had stopped the car in front of her house. He waited, not offering to assist her as in the past. Sharon's voice held vehemence and certainty. Her fingers pressed on his hand. He did not stir. The touch of her hand was almost unbearable in its sweetness and comfort. He tried to keep his hand very still so that she would not become aware that her hand was holding his.

He sighed heavily. "Thanks, Sharon."

Sharon sat down on a kitchen chair trembling and close to tears. Robert would be home soon. She made an effort to compose herself and face the emptiness of the room.

After work the following evening, Sharon threaded her way down the street, taking pains to avoid the melting slushy snow. She did not go directly to her bus stop but went instead to the flower shop and bought a bouquet of colored daises. When she reached the Christian Home she went directly to the desk and inquired, "I am here to see Mary Simon. Would you be so kind as to give me her room number or point her out to me?" She looked around the sitting room and wondered which of the ladies in wheelchairs might be Nathan's mother.

"Mary is the lady by the window with the checker board." Mary absently pushed checkers around the board.

"Hello, Mary, I am Nathan Van Veer's secretary. My name is Sharon."

Oh, you know my Jonny? Nathan is his business name. He is an important lawyer. One day he showed me and Patty his office."

"Yes. He is a good lawyer. I work for him. See, I brought you some flowers."

"For me, and today is not even Friday." Mary giggled and pushed her face into the flowers. "Thank you."

"You are very pretty, Mary."

"Jonny says I am pretty. Will you play checkers with me? The nurses are too busy. My daddy used to play checkers with me, but he is in heaven now. Sometimes Jonny plays, but I always beat him. Mostly, he takes me out to lunch and we do not have time to play checkers."

Sharon sat at the table across from Mary. "I like the red ones," said Mary.

"Good, then I will take the black. I have not played checkers in a long time."

Mary pushed a checker. "Now it is your move."

Sharon found it difficult to concentrate. All this time, she imagined Nathan's mother to be crippled. This lady's handicap was mental. She could see why Nathan lover her simple charm.

"I beat. I beat Jonny's girlfriend," chanted Mary. "Jonny has two girl friends, Patty and Sharon."

"You sure did beat me. I was not watching closely enough. But, you must not call me Jonathan's girlfriend. He would not like it. I work for him. Please, call me Sharon. Okay?"

"Bye, Sharon. Come back and play checkers again?"

"Yes, Mary, I will come again. Good-bye."

Events of the day occupied Sharon's mind. No wonder Nathan felt so distraught over his grandparents' death. They acted as his parents, now he must act as a parent to his mother.

Nathan wearily climbed the steps to his apartment. A feeling of lassitude overwhelmed him. Molehills became mountains. He never quite caught up with all his work. The burden of his practice produced strain enough, but extra hours of research took their toll. Since childhood, he carried a weight of anger. Only recently, did he have means to do anything about it. Nathan's law degree and his association with Van De and Van Dann, now finally his own law office, were a prelude to his final efforts of revenge.

Every spare moment, Nathan researched old newspaper files. A friend in the police department checked back records of rape cases, but found no trace of Nathan's father. He never let anyone know enough of his plan of battle to get an idea of the whole. He believed this type of crime would surface again. However, Dr. Perkins' warning words came flooding back to him. "This might not be so in your father's case. Your father was my friend and not the usual criminal. Pushed beyond his limits, he cracked under the pressure."

Nathan thought, *I know about pressure.* Bitterness brushed its finger across Nathan's face. *I have lived a long time with pressure. When I find the man who begat me without a thought of nurturing as a father, I will pressure him with a vengeance. Statute of limitations may have run out once. But the next time there will be no mercy. Meanwhile, I must content myself with seeking justice for my clients.*

A knock at the door interrupted Nathan's thought. "Have you eaten supper?" Mrs. Dyke placed a warm casserole in Nathan's hands. "A fine supper buries the burdens of the day," she said.

"Thank you. Sometimes I forget about eating. But you should not worry about me."

"It is the mother in me. I need to worry about someone, and with Ellen away—besides, what would people think if I let you starve? My! You do look tired. Here, you sit. I will fix you a plate. Then you better get some rest?" Mrs. Dyke went to the kitchen and soon came back with a plate for Nathan. She set it in front of him and went back downstairs to where her husband slept in front of the television. The house was too quiet.

Nathan rarely watched television. He scanned the morning *Press* while consuming his coffee that he drank to keep himself propelled throughout the day. Mrs. Dyke was right about one thing. He needed to get more rest. But she could not know how difficult he found it.

Strange dreams left Nathan more tired in the morning than when he went to bed. Again, he was a little boy searching for his father in a crowd at the fair. But he only saw his grandfather's face. Just as he reached him who he supposed was his father, he disappeared into the crowd. Wild hawkers tugged at him to come and play their games of skill and win a prize. He wanted no prize, only his grandfather, or perhaps his father.

Nathan awoke trembling and covered with perspiration. He read awhile before trying to go back to sleep. But, dreams continued to plague him, while rest evaded him.

Oh, how he missed his grandparents. He tried to convince himself that he sought justice for his grandparents' sake as well as for his mother and himself. The thought of justice against his father seemed less important now. Now that possibility eluded him, Nathan considered whether he sought justice or revenge. His grandparents, no longer affected by the outcome, had forgiven Martin Van Vedder long ago.

Chapter Twenty

The arrival of spring did not lift Nathan's spirits. A depression heavier than the proverbial millstone settled down on his shoulders. He lost weight. Sharon often heard him sigh over his work. Nathan glared at the clock. Each click of the minute had snapped at his nerves. His attitude was taking its toll on Sharon. No matter what she did, he was never satisfied. Her patience was draining. She had to talk to him. With a pounding heart, she knocked his door.

"Enter," he said abruptly.

As Sharon dawdled by the door, he motioned her to a chair. She sat on the edge of her chair, her face reddened. "I have to tell you something." He nodded for her to continue.

"Your attitude of late makes me tense. I think I am a good secretary, but if you want me to do things differently you will have to tell me. I think I deserve the same respect you give your clients."

Color drained from his face. An old familiar picked-on feeling gnawed at his stomach. He looked bewildered. After an interval he replied with regret, "I was not aware I was being so disagreeable. I will try to be more civil."

It was a difficult apology to make. A sliver of a smile pierced his sad face.

Sharon smiled and her face brightened as she arose from her chair. "Thanks." She went back to her office and worked with renewed vigor.

Nathan squared his shoulders. She had accepted his apology. How could he have burdened her with his problems? But had he ruined any chances of ever winning her love? He was torn between doubt, torture and hope. Work proceeded automatically for a while, but grief still bound Nathan. Sharon had faced him once. She felt she must try again.

Sharon put her name on Nathan's appointment calendar for late in the day. "Come in. Please sit down." He leaned back in his chair. "How may I help you?" He supposed she had a legal problem. Sharon cringed at the familiar face filled to sagging with sadness.

Sharon looked directly at Nathan. "What if my father refuses to make a will?"

"Is he refusing?"

"No. But would not our interest automatically be taken care of, even if we did nothing?"

Nathan looked at her quizzically. "Well, many times things taken care of by others do not meet everyone's satisfaction."

"Nathan, my friend, you may not consider me very polite, but you do not take your own advice." Her words had the effect of a neatly thrown grenade.

"What do you mean by that?" he challenged, leaning forward.

Sharon had started something. She must pursue. "You have just informed me how important it is to get matters settled. I understand your grief, because of my own. But, you must will yourself to get on with your life. Do not let your grief keep you from working to attain your goals in life."

"Are you saying that I am not doing my job? You have no idea of my life goals."

"You are going through the motions of doing your work, but your heart is not in it." He knew she spoke the truth. He had no answer. He was afraid to look for joy in his life.

"God can comfort you as he does me," she said softly, laying a gentle hand on his arm. Nathan sat with bowed head, locked in a strange silence. Shattered remnants of thoughts raced through his mind. Her touch gave him courage to look up. Tears glistened in his eyes. "I wonder if there will ever be pleasure again in living?" He surprised himself with this admission to her.

"There will be," she assured him.

"All I can feel now is anger and an alien numbness. I never knew my father. Now, his surrogate, Grandfather, has been wrenched from me. And Grandmother, mother to my mother and myself, her life needlessly cut short." Racking sobs shook him, releasing his grief for the first time. Sharon prayed quietly. Tears meant that now his burden was bearable.

When his sobs ceased, she spoke. "God understands our losses. His only Son died on the cross for the sins of each of us. He lives again in heaven and will live in us, if we open our hearts to accept him." Vaguely, Nathan remembered similar words spoken by his grandfather and felt a little closer to him. For once, he did not object to her mention of God.

"Nathan, come to our house for dinner this evening. You need not talk. Just be with people who care about you. You need nourishment and rest. Neglecting yourself will cause you to lose court cases. That is not a good reputation for an up-and-coming brilliant lawyer." So, she still had faith in him, he thought.

"You are right. I must pull myself together. I cannot afford to lose my law practice, if I plan on taking care of Mother. I am not even good company for her."

"Your mother seems to be doing fine. I visit her at least once a week and Patty visits her also. Your friends want to help you."

Touched by her concern, he arose. "I think a good meal might be just what I need. No reflection on Mrs. Dyke's casseroles."

"Well, let's go. Father and Robert will be glad to see you."

"You make it difficult to refuse."

"I hope I have made it impossible." She smiled up at him and took his arm.

A tempting aroma greeted them as they entered the Reid home.

"Father, Robert, we have company. Make yourself comfortable, Nathan. I will be back in a minute."

"Welcome company indeed," said Mr. Reid, coming from the kitchen. Nathan listened to his friend discuss the events of the day and absorbed the warmth of the family around him as he had at his grandparents' home. Their calmness of spirit and encouragement soothed his tattered nerves. A hope began to build within him, though his grandparents could never be replaced.

Chapter Twenty-One

Mary awoke early with the sun streaming in her window. She hurried out of bed. "Today is Easter," she sang. "Miss Sharon and Jonny are going to take me to church." Mary used to attend with her parents, but now they were celebrating in heaven.

Mary put on her new Easter dress and gloves to match. "Hi, Jonny, I am ready." She beamed with excitement.

"Hi, Mom," He bent and kissed her cheek and smiled at her cheerfulness.

"Aren't you excited, Jonny?"

"Maybe I am a little. I am kind of nervous. Time stretches long between Christmas and Easter." He thought of the time he attended with Patty and remained unmoved. But, he rather enjoyed the Children's Christmas program he attended with Sharon. He followed the Christmas story of the shepherds, angels and wise men. He felt the excitement he remembered as a child.

"You look beautiful today, Mom."

"So do you." Nathan wore his best pinstripe suit that he saved for special occasions to impress the judge or jury. Mary sat beside her handsome son. She was happy that he agreed to accompany her and Sharon today. Nathan surveyed the simple church and the sincere, friendly people. Sharon gave him an encouraging smile. Organ music provided a peaceful background for the murmur of voices as people were ushered to their pews.

The congregation stood to sing "He Lives." Nathan's baritone blended with Sharon's clear soprano. Robert found the page and shared a book with Mary, who joined in heartily on the chorus.

Sharon sang a solo. Nathan searched her face and basked in her pleasure as she sang, "He is Risen." He did not hear or remember much of the rest of the service. His mind focused on Sharon and the words of her song. He felt a glimmer of hope.

On the way home from church, Sharon and Robert told Nathan about their weekly Bible study. "I am afraid I have not done much Bible reading," admitted Nathan.

"Mother read the Bible to me," said Mary.

"Grandmother read her Bible faithfully every day," Nathan agreed.

"Each of us needs to read the Bible and understand for ourselves," said Robert.

"The Bible is a history of Israel and Judah. Scientific discoveries back the story of creation of the world. All of which should be of interest to a legal mind such as yours. Besides, the Bible contains stories, poetry, songs of praise, proverbs for daily living, explorations of strong men, stories of men who fell short and of God's forgiving love," added Sharon.

"You make the Bible sound interesting, but my mind only absorbs and functions effectively when not on overload. Presently, it is dangerously near full capacity." So, they dropped the matter. Nathan doubted his own hope for a future life when this life was so confused. Perhaps, he was too self-centered to be forgiven by God.

Sharon had prepared a lovely dinner that the friends shared together. Afterwards, Robert entertained Mary with a game of checkers. Sharon tidied up the kitchen.

Nathan went to look for Sharon and found her gazing at an Easter lily absorbed in thought. When he perceived her expression he would have gone away, feeling that he was trespassing on a private moment. But she turned at the sound of his footstep. He noticed a tear in her eye. "What is it?" he asked, stepping forward and drawing her into his arms.

"Oh, Nathan," she sighed, leaning her head on his shoulder, yielding to his embrace. "I miss my mother so much. Oh, I know I will see her again someday. But today, my heart is heavy." Sharon clung to him a moment, then pulled away. "I should be comforting you on the loss of your grandparents."

He buried his face in her soft hair and murmured, "I love you, Sharon. I have loved you since that first day you came to my office." Sharon lifted her face to look at Nathan. He kissed her tenderly on the lips. "Now that I have put into words what I have felt so long, is my love an insult to you?"

"Any woman would be honored by such a love as yours," she answered. "But, I need time."

Chapter Twenty-Two

"Hello, Father. How are you today?" asked David.

"I would feel better if I were not attached to all these tubes," Mark Wagner replied. "This heart attack makes me weak. I am a tired old man."

David held his father's once-firm hand in his. "I am glad you asked God into your life before you became ill the first time."

"Yes, God allowed me time to make peace with Him. I want to thank you, Son, for sharing your faith with me. Without your exuberant belief in God's love, I would not know God still loved me. I am sorry I drove your mother away with my drinking. I need to ask your forgiveness now, that I have found God's forgiveness."

"I forgave you, Dad, when God forgave me and His love entered my life."

"Son, there is one other thing I should have straightened out. My time is limited. I need your help."

"I am listening. But do not tire yourself out."

"David. There is no easy way to tell you this. So, I shall just state the facts. I hope you can forgive me." Mark closed his eyes in a silent prayer before continuing. "David, my son, you have a brother." David did not believe he heard correctly.

"Say that again, Dad."

"You have an older brother. I want you to find him and include him in any inheritance, whatever may be left after my expenses are paid."

David started to say something, but his father lifted his hand to silence him. "It happened a long while ago, before I met your mother. When I heard the girl was pregnant, I got scared and left town. I was a coward. I even changed my name."

"I returned to my hometown once and saw her in the yard with her small son. Guilt and shame have been my companions since. That is why I always drank on your birthdays. Every time I looked at you I thought of the child I dared not love. But I could not pretend he did not exist."

"What is his name?" asked David. But his father's breath became short and he could not respond. Nurses and doctors swarmed around Mark. Stunned, David stood in the corridor trying to comprehend what his father told him."

A nurse directed David back to his father's room. "I am sorry. We did everything possible. Perhaps, you would like a little time alone with your father. May I call someone for you?"

"Just call my wife. Tell her I will be home in a little while."

David often wished for a brother. Now, when he was about to find one, his father was gone. David felt alone and cheated. The next few days were filled with funeral preparations. David pushed aside his own problems. But one day as David and Anne sat quietly looking over cards of condolences David took a deep breath and told Anne, "Just before Dad died he made the strangest confession. He said I have an older brother and would I please try to find him. I hardly know where to begin. Dad also said that he changed his name. Can you imagine that?"

"Oh, David," said Anne, putting her arms around him. "No wonder you have been so troubled. All of this happened when you and your father were getting along so well."

The next morning David kissed Anne good-bye. "Thanks for understanding, dear."

David made me stop at the courthouse. He checked records but found nothing. Dad had never been one to talk about his family background, only that his parents died a long time ago. Finally, David remembered Dad's treasured wooden box. Mark never allowed anyone to touch it. "I still remember Dad's anger the first time I tried to look in it," he told Anne. Cautiously, David lifted the little box out of a larger, locked box. He seated himself in his Dad's old rocking chair and thumbed through a stack of old photos of strangers. One picture looked like his dad as a young man. Beside him an elderly couple stood, probably his parents. Turning the photo over, David found not his dad's name, but the name of a Martin Van Vedder. Could this be a cousin? He searched the other photos, all Van Vedder, perhaps his family name before Dad changed it.

Then David came across citizenship papers, a marriage license and a birth certificate of a child, Martin Van Vedder. Well, the birth date coincided with his father's birthday. The name of the place of birth was Cascade. Never before had David been called upon to bear this kind of pain. Hope was the thing that prodded him on. David had always thought of himself a particular person with a certain name. Now, he found out to the contrary. So many things changed.

David wondered, *Did Dad ever love me as a child? What will my brother be like? More to the point, will my brother accept me as a brother?*

David drove until he came to the little town. There he found a clinic and they directed him to old Dr. Perkins, a longtime resident of the town. David walked up the worn path to knock at the doctor's door. He began to have second thoughts about unlocking the past. *But no, Dad requested this unknown brother be included in the will. I must honor his request.*

I must assure my brother of Dad's love and beg his forgiveness. David was about to turn away when the door creaked open.

"Hello, Dr. Perkins?"

"Yes."

"My name is David Wagner. I came to find some information about my father. The clinic referred me to you. Dad passed away last week and it may help me if I can find out a little about my roots."

"Come in." He motioned David to a seat. "I am sorry about your father. What did you say your name was again?"

"David Wagner."

"I do not believe I know of any Wagners."

"Oh, I think Dad mentioned he changed his name when he left here. An embarrassing situation with a young lady caused him to run away. I would like to find my brother. This may be a picture of my dad as a young man. And here is a birth certificate and citizenship papers I found in his box. The name says Van Vedder. I wonder if that could have been my father's name?"

Dr. Perkins' hands shook. He eagerly took the picture and gazed at it. He had waited years to hear news of this friend. "Yes." He nodded to himself, my old friend.

"My, my, I have not heard this name in years. We were good friends." Dr. Perkins hesitated, wondering how best to tell David of his father's past. "So," he said, "Tell me about your father. How was he?"

"The last few months my father and I shared some good times. When I was young he drank a lot. We lived in the southern part of the state. After my mother left us, we moved to the city. I became a Christian a year ago and my father found God last Thanksgiving."

"I am glad to hear that. I hope what I have to tell you will not lessen your love for your father. When Martin was a young man, he helped his parents build the house, here in the photo. It is just down the street. Martin was the best carpenter in town. His parents died. And shortly after that his fiancée was struck and killed by a drunk driver. Martin was dumped into a dungeon of depression. For a brief time, he seemed to be better. Then one day, a young girl on this street walked by. In his confusion and passion, he must have thought she was his fiancée. He raped her."

Dr. Perkins paused to let the significance of his last statement sink into David's consciousness.

"Rape, my father, are you sure?"

"I confronted him after examining the girl. He made no move to deny it. The next morning, he disappeared. I found his driver's license on the porch."

David found it difficult to absorb this news. His father had not mentioned rape. He remembered his father was not a Christian when he was a young man. Satan delights in working his wickedness through those serving him. Aloud, he said, "So that is why my father ran away."

"Yes. I am also a friend of the girl's family. They were devastated and the girl's father enraged. I agreed to talk to Martin and see if he would take some responsibility. The next morning he was gone. I have been looking after his place ever since, hoping he would return."

"You say they live on this street? I am anxious to meet them. My father asked God's forgiveness and wanted to include his other child in his will. I would like to ask their forgiveness for my father. He died before he could give me any details or names." David, anxious to get this business behind him, fidgeted in his chair.

"Things may not be that simple. Your brother has had years of anger building up. I think he planned revenge, if he ever found his father. Now, he may seek to hurt you now that possibility has been taken from him by your father's death. Perhaps, it would be better to let the matter drop."

David considered, but decided, "It is my Christian duty to confess for my father and try to make amends. Besides, a brother might be just what I need. Will you please tell me how to find him?"

"I will give you the information. You would be proud to call this young man your brother. But, remember the circumstances of his birth. His anger has been building for a long time. Perhaps I could help defuse the situation before you spring it on him." Again, Dr. Perkins found himself a link between the families.

"That might be a good idea. However, I am most anxious to meet my brother." Dr. Perkins leaned forward and spoke distinctly to David. "Your brother's name is Jonathan Simon."

"Jonathan Simon," David repeated.

"Yes. But now he goes by a different name. He is a lawyer in the city. You may have heard of him. Nathan Van Veer. He shortened the Van Vedder name."

David's face registered shock. "Know him! We are friends. We play chess with a mutual friend, Robert Reid."

"Is he the Robert Reid who recently dated my granddaughter, Patty?"

"Patty Perkins. Well, I'll be. Robert's sister Sharon works for Nathan," said David.

"Do you by any chance know Sharon and Robert's father's name?"

"I think his name is Frank," answered David.

"It was Frank Reid's sister, Suzanne, who was engaged to Martin before her untimely death."

"My father and Frank met recently, but neither hinted of being former acquaintances. Of course my father changed his name and time has a way of altering appearances."

Both men tried to absorb all that just transpired between them. A new fear gripped David. *What if Nathan hates me for this? Can I risk losing a friend, perhaps even Robert and Sharon's friendship?*

Dr. Perkins interrupted his thoughts. "Did Jonathan or Nathan ever meet your father?"

David considered a moment. "I think they met a couple of times at my place."

"The next question I have for you: Have you met Nathan's mother?"

"I met her briefly at the Easter service. She was with Nathan and the Reids."

"Then you know she suffers retardation. It was an accident at her birth when the cord became entangled around her neck and she did not get enough oxygen. She and Nathan are very devoted to each other. The loss of her parents has been difficult for both of them.

"David, I am happy to make your acquaintances, if for no other reason than to know what became of my long-lost friend. I regret his demise. I had hoped to see him again. Please give my regards to Frank Reid when you see him again. Now, we need to make plans to enlighten Nathan of your relationship. I hope he chooses to let you be his brother. You seem like a nice young man. I have kept Martin and his son Jonathan in my prayers all these years."

Chapter Twenty-Three

Nathan asked, "What do I owe this honor? An old friend and a new one wish to see me simultaneously." They shook hands.

Dr. Perkins cleared his throat, looked over his spectacles first at David, then Nathan. "Jonathan, I know you have been searching for your father for some time now. David has some interesting news for us."

"Well, out with it. Don't keep me waiting in suspense, and why didn't he come to me first?" Nathan looked at David.

"It seems David's father used to live in our town before David was born."

"Did he know my father?"

Dr. Perkins nodded then went on. "Nathan, your father changed his name and identity when he left. David found some pictures and addresses while going through some of his father's things."

"Why didn't you come to me?" Nathan urged again.

"He did not know," Dr. Perkins answered for him. Nathan looked at David, but David kept his gaze fastened on Dr. Perkins.

"Did you identify the pictures? Was it my father? Where is he now? I would like to see the photo."

"Sorry. It is just that I have waited so long," said Nathan.

"The picture is of your father and his parents in front of their home. But I am afraid your father died recently."

"Not now!" Nathan flinched as if physically struck. His face whitened and he gripped the arms of his chair. He had not expected this. "Why? I came so close to finding him. How dare he do this to me on top of everything else?"

Dr. Perkins laid a hand on Nathan's shoulder. "It seems I have only been the bearer of bad news for you lately."

"It is not your fault. You are caught in the middle. But how do you know my father is dead?"

Dr. Perkins returned to his seat and sighed heavily. He took a moment to collect his wits and gave David a look of sympathy before answering.

"Jonathan, it seems the man in the picture, your father, was also David's father."

Nathan rose in a rage and David shrank back. "Why didn't you tell me you were my brother? You came around here pretending to be my friend. Get out! I hate you for what your father did to me and my mother."

"I did not know he was your father until I went to see Dr. Perkins trying to find out about my father. I am still your friend. I am truly sorry for my father's actions. But I am not sorry it is you who are my brother."

"Liar!" stormed Nathan.

"Jonathan," said Dr. Perkins quietly. "Look at the picture. The man in the picture is the same as in the picture that I gave you years ago. Now, look at each other. David is taller with lighter hair, but you both possess that same strong, deeply dimpled chin."

"David, tell me if your father had any distinguishing marks."

"He had a dark birthmark on his right knee," answered David.

"Pull up your pant leg, Jonathan," ordered Dr. Perkins with the authoritative voice of tough professionalism. Shocked with disbelief, Nathan obediently started to raise his pant leg. Then he changed his mind. He yanked down on his pant leg and stalked out of his office. The door slammed behind him. An astonished Sharon looked up as a grim-faced Nathan passed her desk. Sharon hugged herself as if suddenly chilled.

Nathan drove for hours. He thought he had been toughened by pain in his youth, but he was unprepared for this. After all the years of planning how he would someday find his father and watch him in a courtroom as a jury pronounced him guilty and the judge sentenced him, victory was snatched away. How dare he die? Nathan hoped his father had suffered guilt all his life. Nathan's house of cards had fallen. And how was he supposed to feel about David?

Meanwhile, Dr. Perkins told David, "Give him time. He has suffered a shock. Justice or any hope of knowing his father has just been denied him. I hope you can one day be brothers."

Dr. Perkins drove back to his home with heaviness of heart. He had done his part in mentoring Nathan and watching over the Van Vedder place. His efforts in the reconciliation of his friend's sons seemingly had little effect. But, he was content that he had glimpsed his friend Martin again briefly in his son David.

Nathan returned to his room and took out his pipe for a smoke. Then, he thrust it from him. He wanted no part of his father now. But he could not resist taking out the worn picture of his father and studying it again. Could they be mistaken? His eyes burned and his head throbbed. Nothing made sense. He wondered what made him most angry? Was he angry that Mark had not revealed who he was when they met years ago or recently when they met again? A thing Nathan had dreaded had happened. He was more a part of his father than he realized. They were both caught up in a web of deceit.

Nathan remembered the love he saw between David and his father, Mark. He still could not call him his own father. Perhaps, if he had disliked Mark when they met at Van De's he would have vented some of his anger on his father then. And, he did not understand his anger towards David, who was innocent. Nathan felt betrayed. He and David had been friends. How could they act like brothers? What could they share now that their father was gone? Nathan turned out the lights and lay in bed tossing and turning unable to sleep. Tomorrow he would call Sharon and tell her that he would not be in the office for a few days. He had some things to tend to.

Anne had called Sharon to prepare her and let her know about the discovery of Nathan's father and that Nathan and David were brothers.

"Hello, Mother," David greeted Jenny. "I am glad you came. You must meet your grandson, Mark."

"Do come in," Anne had met Jenny once before at the occasion of David's and her wedding.

"What a handsome little fellow," said Jenny. "He looks like David when he was a baby." To the baby she said, "I am your grandma and I love you." Little Mark responded by cooing and holding tightly to her finger.

David and his mother sat in the kitchen drinking coffee while Anne put the baby to bed. "I understand why you did not come to Dad's funeral," said David. "But I am glad you came to see me now. Dad said some strange things before he died that I want to discuss with you."

"Your dad and I were so in love when we first married. But ghosts lived in him, condemning and unconsoling. After you were born, he started drinking. It was so unlike him. I should not have nagged him about it, but I felt helpless. I know he loved you."

"I know he loved me at the end, but things were different when I was growing up. Dad said he was sorry that he hurt you. But you will never believe what he told me." David paused and looked at his mother. "Before you and Dad were married, he had a son. I just found out who he was. He and I know each other. But now, things are all mixed up. It will take a while to work things out. His name is Nathan. He resents Dad and me. He thought I pretended to be his friend and did not tell him we were brothers. I hope we can be good friends again. It will take away some of the hurt of losing Dad. I can understand a little how my brother feels, never having a father.

"I traced Dad through some of his papers in his locked box. Dr. Perkins told me that first, Dad's parents died. Then he lost his fiancée in an accident. I guess he was pretty depressed and in shock. The hard thing to believe is that in this state of mind he thought his neighbor girl was his fiancée and he raped her. The girl was retarded, a birth injury. Her son, my brother, is now a fine lawyer. In fact he was driven to become a lawyer so he could bring Dad to justice, if he ever found him. I wanted you to know the whole truth. This has haunted Dad. He was afraid to tell you for fear of losing you, too. All he managed to do was drive you away," David said.

Jenny wiped at a tear. "I wish I had known."

Chapter Twenty-Four

David spent half the next day with fingers hovered over the telephone almost deciding to ring up Nathan. Instead he went to visit him. He breathed a prayer as he pushed the doorbell. Nathan appeared almost immediately. "Clear out or I will throw you out," he threatened.

"Well, I will be travelling so you do not have to mess up your place throwing me out, but please, we need to talk. Please, Nathan, we were friends." Nathan relented and allowed David to enter.

"Thanks. I am sorry you have been hurt. But I also lost a father."

"I do not need your sympathy," Nathan muttered.

"May we sit down?" asked David.

"Suit yourself." Nathan continued to puff on his pipe, the echo of a grudge still strong.

David sat in the nearest chair, feeling rather shaky. "I had no idea my dad had done anything criminal. I feel doubly hurt and confused knowing that this hurt you. As friends we need to find a way to help ourselves get over this. I know you were searching for a father not a brother, but neither of us has much family. You liked Dad when you met him at Van D's and when you met him again as my dad. What different would you expect from him when he did not know who you were?"

Nathan tipped his chair recklessly backward. He finally let his weight fall forward with a thud. "I do not know. I never knew what to expect from a father. I pictured someone quite different. I had Grandfather Simon. I guess, I just wanted someone of my own."

"Not someone who had a younger brother attached to it, huh?" said David. "I sure could use a big brother now."

Nathan laughed aloud. "Now that's a new role for me." Each sat lost in their thoughts. Finally Nathan offered, "Would you like a cup of coffee?" That is the least he would have done for a stranger.

"That would be fine." Maybe they were getting somewhere. Nathan studied David over his coffee cup, his agitation turned to concentration. Strange, how he unwillingly was drawn to him.

"Perhaps, we could start over as friends." suggested David.

"I am having trouble thinking logically as a lawyer should," Nathan admitted. "We should try to fit the pieces of our lives together. Dr. Perkins filled us in on Father's life, before I was born. You can supply what happened after that."

David nodded. "I remember my fifth birthday. Dad missed my party. He came home late, drunk. I guess he was thinking about you."

"I remember my first day of school," said Nathan, his voice vibrating. "Grandmother and Mother took me. The kids laughed at my mother and I punched one of them. It was the first time I felt different."

"I used to get in trouble in school for fighting," said David. "I had one special friend, Hal. We liked to wrestle. But, when one got rough, the other ended up fighting for real until the teacher broke us apart."

"What about high school? Did you date any pretty girls?" asked David.

"Patty Perkins was and still is my faithful friend, even if she is a year older than me. I avoided other girls as much as possible."

"I did too. Girls did not like my friends. Looking back, they were not the best company. We moved to this city after my mother left. I barely made it through school. I missed my mother," said David. As an afterthought he said, "I like your mother, Nathan. Does that surprise you?"

"In a way, I always loved her. Sometimes, it was difficult to understand when people made fun of her."

David almost felt like the elder brother trying to make peace. Besides, he had always had his father, the father Nathan could not find. Yet, David looked up to Nathan, a respected lawyer. To Nathan he said, "I almost envy you the close relationship you had with your mother and grandparents."

"I think Grandfather would have been happy if I had stayed around and worked with him. He always said I worked well with my hands."

David looked at his watch. He was not sure how to progress with this conversation. Some things were still too painful to discuss. "Anne will be waiting for me," he said and stood to leave. "Thanks for letting me in."

A few days later, David received a surprise visit from Nathan. "I have something to show you. I found this carving at the Van Vedder place when Patty and I played there."

David's eyebrows raised. "Let me see that. I have one exactly like it. Wait." He returned with a duplicate carving, a wooden chain of identical boxes. Each box contained a wooden ball floating in the center space, the whole thing carved from one piece of wood.

"This may be what we have been searching for to link Jonathan Simon, Martin Van Vedder and David Wagner together as a family," suggested Nathan. "I always wondered how those balls got into the boxes."

"So did I," confessed David. "They are as complex as our family."

"There is one other thing that Dr. Perkins mentioned that I think you should know. Perhaps, you better sit down for this one," said David pulling out a chair for his brother.

"Our father, Martin Van Vedder, was engaged to a Suzanne Reid before her death. She was none other than the sister of Frank Reid and aunt to Sharon and Robert."

Nathan's jaw dropped. He threw up his hands in disbelief. "Well," was all he could manage to say. Grandfather had mentioned that he would one day discover he inherited a positive characteristic from his father. Of course, if his father had married Suzanne, he and Sharon would be cousins. He preferred it not to be that way.

David and Nathan arrived at the ballpark as a group of Little Leaguers assembled on a Saturday morning. Nathan had agreed to come along, as he wanted to get out of the house before Ellen arrived to visit her parents. This also provided a way to get to know David better.

David had become friends with Tommy and Sam, who lived on his block. They did not mind that David cheered for everyone regardless of their fumbles, not like their demanding fathers or frenzied mothers. David remembered his own Little League days, but his father did not have time or inclination to watch him play. Occasionally, his mother watched and he played with all his might.

Nathan never received an invitation to play the coveted game. However, he and Patty often watched from their perch in the apple tree. Today, the parade of boys courageously swung the bat again and again. Disregarding skinned knees, they raced around the bases and slid into home base. Those who struck out or were tagged gave forlorn, furtive glances over their shoulders for a sign of approval.

Harsh words broke their revelry. The umpire stood aghast as two mothers railed accusations at him. One would have thought the umpire had made a decision against them personally.

"We have a lawyer here, better not incriminate yourselves," called David, giving Nathan a nudge with his elbow. The women shot glaring looks in their direction.

"Poor little fellows," said Nathan. "The boys are like pawns in a chess game."

After a couple more outs, Sam and Tommy ran up to David. "I only made one out today," beamed Tommy.

"Did you see my home run?" interrupted Sam.

"You fellows were great," said David. "How would you like to stop for ice cream on the way home?"

"Oh boy, that sounds cool to me," said Sam and they all laughed.

"Wait," said Nathan. "I see a couple friends of mine. Hey, Josh and George, want to go for ice cream with us?" he called to his black neighbor's children.

"Thank you, Mr. V. But you will have to explain to Mama if we are late."

"We will brave her all together," he said. The boys chattered happily about each one's accomplishments of the day. Somehow, David and Nathan felt they were regaining a part of their lost boyhood.

Chapter Twenty-Five

Nathan stepped lightly along the sidewalk through the rain trying not to get his feet wet. He did not want to appear bedraggled when he arrived. He was ushered into a conference room much larger than his office. Mr. Van De pushed himself up as Nathan approached. Nathan held out his hand that the other shook warmly. David and Dr. Perkins were seated across from Mr. Van De. Van De clasped his hands across his stomach with an air of thoughtful authority. He could be as sympathetic with a genuine problem as he was tough with deadbeats.

Dr. Perkins confirmed that the pictures of David's father were the same as Nathan's father, Martin Van Vedder. He also produced Nathan's birth records where Martin was listed as father and birthmark noted.

David gave an account of his father's deathbed confession. Since there was no contesting of the will, Van De was pleased to present to Nathan a part of his past with hope for the future.

"Sign here. Your father's house now belongs to you." How strange to hear these words, father, brother. How he would have liked to hear them as a child.

"Here is the deed to your house." David handed him the paper, then embraced him. Legally, they were family. Nathan reimbursed Dr. Perkins for taxes that he paid through the years. David sold Mark's other house and paid medical and funeral expenses. The remaining assets were his.

Cynthia was stunned when she heard the news that Nathan had found his father and that David was his brother. She had a premonition that now Nathan had found his family, he never would become a part of hers. She liked David and Anne well enough, but they did not circulate in the same social strata. However, Cynthia was glad that Nathan was moving farther away from Sharon. He would be closer to Patty, but Cynthia did not worry about her. She and Nathan were childhood friends, nothing more. As for Ellen, Cynthia considered her out of sight, out of mind. But Ellen was more optimistic as Nathan promised to have dinner with her again before he moved.

Sharon rejoiced with Nathan. "God gave you a new family, after you lost your grandparents."

"It is hardly the same," Nathan said sadly.

"David and Anne can be a great help to you if you will let them," said Sharon. She prayed that their faith might eventually lead Nathan to trust God. With Nathan living out of the city, she need only face him at work. He and Robert would not be getting together so often to play chess. It would be easier for Sharon to hide her feelings from Nathan. She reproved herself for thinking he loved her. But, she could not forget the look in his eyes when he held her and confessed his love to her last Easter. His demeanor remained as it always had been at work, professional. He resolved he would not ever cause Sharon embarrassment.

Nathan studied the piece of paper in his hand. He had never had a home, only with his grandparents. It had been a while since anyone lived there, but Dr. Perkins reassured him that his house was still in good repair. Nathan decided to drive out and see the property for himself and come to terms with his father.

Nathan toured the dusty house and tried to envision his grandparents and father living here. Could he bring his mother to live in this house? Would she be afraid of it? He hoped he would be comfortable back in his old neighborhood commuting to work. The Dykes had been good to Nathan and his mother was reasonably comfortable in the Christian Home, but they looked forward to being together again. He would hire someone to stay with his mother. Nathan sat in his grandfather's chair. He closed his eyes. Words came to him from the Easter message; Words of the Heavenly Father's love and the sacrifice of his Son, so men could be brothers. Nathan had learned to love his brother David for what he unselfishly did for him. Was this what Grandfather Simon tried to tell him all these years?

"Father, Father," Nathan repeated, letting the beauty of the words erase the bitterness from his soul. Nathan dozed in the big chair for some time, but awoke refreshed. It was getting dark and he needed to head back to the city.

The next morning, Nathan arrived at his office early. He needed to see Sharon. When Sharon arrived, Nathan called her to his office. "I have something to tell you. Last night I went to my new home and made peace with my father. Also, I want you to know that I made peace with God. My own selfishness looked to me as it must have looked to others all along. I had a good look at myself and did not like what I saw."

"I am happy for you, Nathan, that you have made peace with God and your family."

Nathan reached out to lift her chin and look into her eyes. "Sharon, will you be a part of my family? I love you and want you to be my wife."

"Yes, Nathan. I will." She came to him and they embraced. She lifted her face to him and melted into his kiss.

"If you don't mind waiting a bit to get married, I would like to get mother settled first. Then we can get married and take our time on a honeymoon. I might also, have to look for a new secretary."

"That is all right as long as you don't fall in love with her."

"Not a chance. Wait a minute." Nathan dug in his pocket and pulled out a small box. "I saved Grandmother's ring for you. My mother has her own special jewelry."

"Oh, Nathan, how lovely these are." He placed a ring on her finger then kissed her hand. Then he pulled her into his arms and kissed her again. He reached behind his desk and brought out a beautiful bouquet of roses. She pressed her nose into them and breathed deeply. "So lovely."

"I think we ought to tell our brothers and my father, don't you?" asked Sharon with a big smile.

"How about tonight, after I take you out to dinner."

She nodded in agreement. Just then, someone entered the outer office. "I guess it is time to get to work."

Chapter Twenty-Six

David and Nathan drove along in silence toward the old haunted house, or so it used to be called when Nathan was a child and his grandfather forbade him to go there. "It was a place where evil things happened," he had been told.

"You may find a return to this house too painful under the circumstances. Perhaps, an insult to your pride," said David.

"I cannot afford to be proud, but it is a strange situation," Nathan answered soberly.

Dr. Perkins' goats grazing in the yard looked like demons to children who were superstitious. The goats also worked to deter trespassers. It also kept the yard from taking over the house. Dr. Perkins would sometimes let himself into the house and wander around touching the beautiful woodwork, wondering about his friend. The flicker of his flashlight led townspeople to gossip of haunted houses and evil spirits, spiriting people away.

David let Nathan wander through the house while he walked around the grounds. Columbine grew around an old shed. Hollyhocks brightened a spot under the kitchen windows. Goats grazed on sweet clover. David wished he had known his grandparents. His life would have been different, also. Then, he remembered how it came that his father left this place.

David lingered on the porch until he saw Nathan return from his tour of the house and stand by the fireplace. "Your father had an eye for design," said Nathan.

"Our father," corrected David. "Say, I was almost attacked by your goats outside."

"Serves you right for trespassing," teased Nathan.

"Are you saying I am a poor housekeeper?" said Nathan, giving David a playful punch on the arm. David had been a Christian for some time now, but once in a while old habits caught him off guard. He swung to return Nathan's punch. Nathan caught his arm and before either knew what happened they were wrestling. Each charged with the emotions of the day and past few weeks, clung to the other, whether in a brotherly embrace or resentful over their separation. They struggled, tripped over a chair and rolled on the floor.

Dr. Perkins arrived on the scene in time to see them struggle. "I see the brothers have come home," he chuckled. This brought the young men to the present and they released each other.

"Hi, Doc, we are just trying out what we missed as kids," laughed David. "Hope I did not hurt you, Nathan." They began dusting themselves off.

A few days later, Nathan and David returned with recruits. Patty had enlisted Anne and Sharon's help. They scrubbed the place from stem to stern. "Looks like this place is nearly shipshape," said David. "If you ladies have everything clean, we can move some things in tomorrow. Robert will be free to help with the furniture."

"We will be ready," said Patty. "We scrubbed away the ghosts with the cobwebs." Nathan laughed when he saw the smudge on Patty's face. It reminded him of days when they climbed trees together.

"You look like a little urchin with dirt on your face." He picked her up, twirled her around and planted a kiss on her forehead. The thought of moving into his father's home had made him frolicsome. The girls worked well together and enjoyed the results of setting things to rights.

"Well, let's get busy," he said, suddenly embarrassed. He picked up a rake and watched Patty head toward the house with a tray of empty lemonade glasses. But his eyes were drawn to Sharon arranging a flower box on the porch. She looked up and smiled at him. He was beginning to understand his father's agony in trying to live without his Suzanne if she were anything like Sharon.

Patty blushed and followed Anne and little Mark into the house. She stopped in front of a mirror she had just polished and noted the black smudge on her cheek. She wiped it off with a corner of her apron, then smiled at her reflection. She treasured the kiss Nathan so playfully planted on her. Soon, Nathan would be marrying Sharon.

Patty took the empty glasses into the kitchen. She wondered if this beautiful house was really haunted with the love and spirits of Nathan's forebears.

Nathan and David carried Nathan's grandmother's table into the house and set it in the dining room where it harmonized with the woodwork. They set the Van Vedder chairs up to the table. They chose and arranged furniture. They fixed Mary's room downstairs with her own bed and furniture from her parents' home. Mary's companion would occupy the other downstairs room. Nathan chose the larger room upstairs for a master bedroom and the smaller one for a study.

Finally, Nathan announced, "Time to head back to the city." Nathan opened the front door and motioned to Anne to sit beside her husband. He climbed in back to sit beside Sharon. "You look tired," he said and reached out to draw her closer to him.

"It is a good tired," she said.

Though Nathan wasted most of his younger years planning a strategy of revenge and justice, it was not his effort that located his father. He and David were beginning to feel more like brothers. And, he did appreciate the dramatic transformation that the cleaning had wrought in this beautiful house. His grandfather and Mark, he could not call him Father yet, were skilled craftsmen. Nathan still missed not having a father during his growing-up years, but he could not rewrite history. He had a loving grandfather and Dr. Perkins who tried to fill the gap. But it irritated Nathan that his father died when he was so close to finding him.

Nathan must try now to think of himself as an older brother. He was more knowledgeable in certain matters. However, David had been very fair. Nathan was grateful to him. He would not have blamed David if he had kept the information to himself after his father's death. Their father had lived two lives. Nathan was part of one life and David of another. Now, Sharon had agreed to be his wife.

Chapter Twenty-Seven

Moving day was as exciting for Nathan as it had been for his father when he first moved into this house. Tabby Cat ran ahead of Mary as Nathan held the door for them. Mary was excited to be living with Nathan again. Nathan, a bit uneasy, hurried Mary into the house, not wanting her to focus on the yard until she accepted the house. He was afraid she might remember the trauma of a former day. He wanted his mother to be happy.

Mary stepped inside the big room and went directly to her mother's table. She caressed its fine finish. "Would you like to see the rest of the house?" Patty asked. Longtime acquaintance Patty was the only one there to help her get settled. They toured the kitchen, then the other rooms.

Grandfather Simon's big chair and the Van Vedders' brocaded couch and leather chairs provided a comfortable hodgepodge of furniture reflected in the polished mantel. Fresh flowers filled the house with their aroma.

"Now let's take a look at your room, Mary. I will help you unpack your suitcase and put things away," said Patty. After helping Mary empty her suitcase, she placed it on the shelf from which Martin so long ago removed his.

Nathan brought his suitcases from the car. David would help him get the rest of his belongings from his apartment later. Nathan's bed was made up with one of Grandmother Van Vedder's hand-sewn coverlets. Other linens in the house had been laundered and stored in a hall closet.

Mrs. Dillman arrived. Nathan was glad to obtain her services. This was a big house to care for, and his mother needed company while he worked. Soon, Sharon would be here to keep them all company.

"Hello, Mary." Mrs. Dillman hugged Mary and shook hands with Patty and Nathan. Then she took charge. "Nathan, take my suitcases to my room. Mary, would you like to help me explore the kitchen and find something for your big boy to eat?"

"Okay." Mary was proud of her Jonny and liked to do things for him as any other mother. She set the table while Mrs. Dillman rummaged in the cupboards. After a filling supper the house became quiet. They were satisfied to be home.

-End-